Heart of an Angel

A story about friendship,

dignity, moral courage, and

the many forms

a compassionate heart can take

by

Francis Leung

UNDERCOVER
ANGELS
PUBLISHING

San Francisco Bay Area, California

Heart of an Angel

© 2026 by Francis Leung

Published by Undercover Angels Publishing
San Francisco Bay Area, California

ISBN 979-8-9936455-1-3

Cover design and publisher mark © Undercover Angels Publishing
Printed in the United States of America

First Edition — February 2026

Table of Contents

Preface

This story is not about heroes.

It is about ordinary people placed in moments where strength does not look loud, and love does not look simple. Where courage is measured not by what is taken, but by what is given — or quietly released.

Heart of an Angel is a story about seeing clearly when the world expects blindness, about choosing dignity over dominance, and about the many forms care can take when life does not unfold as planned.

Some of the choices in these pages may seem small. Others may feel costly.

All of them matter.

— *Francis*

Prologue

It is Friday evening.

A middle-aged, muscular man stands in the corner of a street beneath a dim streetlight. A few feet in front of him is a young man in his mid-teens, wearing a bike helmet and a pair of goggles. He faces forward, his whole body rock steady.

They stare at each other in silence for several minutes.

Suddenly, the man lunges forward, his right hand snapping out in a lightning jab aimed at the young man's jaw.

The boy twists his body slightly sideways, the punch grazing past him by inches. At the same time, his right foot lashes out—fast and heavy—but the kick is caught by the man's left palm.

The impact drives the man backward. He stumbles six or seven steps before regaining his balance.

1

The young man steps forward immediately. "Are you okay?" he asks, reaching out his arms.

The man steadies himself and smiles.

"Good job, Charlie."

He grips Charlie's hand in a firm handshake.

"Go sleep early tonight," he says. "You'll need your energy for the battle tomorrow."

~ ~ ~ ~ ~

Chapter 1

Blind Eyes That See

The annual basketball shootout contest among Alameda County high schools is in full swing.

The gymnasium at Sunrise High School is packed to the brim with excited spectators. This year, twelve schools are competing, each sending their top three sharpshooters to the event. On one side, thirty-six skilled players are ready to take their shot, while more than two hundred enthusiastic guests cheer from the stands.

The rules are straightforward: each participant must run along the three-point arc, attempting to score as many baskets as possible within a five-minute time limit. The player with the most successful shots and the best hit-to-miss ratio will be crowned the champion.

In the front row of the stands, a girl in a wheelchair watches a student participant intently through her thick, goggle-like glasses. On the court, a young man wearing identical glasses stands patiently, waiting for his turn.

While the other participants chat among themselves, he remains still, quietly fixated on the basketball hoop without even moving his head.

A fashionable young girl approaches the wheelchair.

"Katie, great to see you again! I was expecting to meet you at the debate contest in a couple of months, but I didn't expect to find you here watching basketball." The girl speaks with enthusiasm. "Who are you rooting for?"

"Hey Krystal, it's Willow Grove versus Einstein again!" Katie replies with a smile. "Your Brandon is Einstein's top shooter, and he's favored to win. I'm here to support my brother."

Krystal follows Katie's gaze and spots the young man with the same goggle-like glasses. "Is that your brother? He is wearing the same type of glasses as you?" she asks.

"Yes, that's him." Katie nods. "I'll tell you the story later."

Katie is a senior in Willow Grove High while Krystal is from the more prestigious Einstein High. They first met during an extramural debate competition, where the Katie-led Willow Grove team triumphed over the Krystal-led Einstein team to win the championship. During the intense competition, the two exchanged sharp, challenging questions but gained a deep respect

4

for each other. Despite their different backgrounds, this respect blossomed into a close friendship.

Katie comes from a single-parent household, with her mother surviving on a modest amount of alimony. Both Katie and her brother Charlie face physical challenges — Katie with cerebral palsy and Charlie who is legally blind. However, thanks to the breakthrough invention of the *Eyes of an Angel* goggles, Katie gradually recovered, and Charlie gained the ability to navigate the world independently.

Krystal's story is quite different. Born into wealth, her parents own both a bank and a department store, and as an only child, she was raised in privilege. Despite these differences, their friendship has thrived, connecting two people from entirely different worlds.

"The next participant is Charlie Santos from Willow Grove," the announcer's voice echoes through the gym.

Charlie steps to the center of the three-point arc, gripping the basketball in both hands. At the sound of the referee's whistle, he begins his routine: shooting, sprinting to retrieve the ball, repositioning on the arc, and shooting again. He may not be the fastest on the court, but his precision is unmatched.

"He's doing really well," Katie observes as she watches closely. "He's a little slower than during practice, but his aim is even sharper."

Krystal nods, impressed. "He's shooting better than most players I've seen in school tournaments. I've been to a lot of matches between Einstein and Willow Grove, but I don't recall seeing him on your basketball team."

Katie smiles. "Joining the basketball team would eat up too much of his study time. Some students can juggle both, but Charlie isn't one of them."

The whistle blows just right after the ball leaves Charlie's hands, and it swishes through the net.

In this competition, scores are revealed only after all participants have finished, a policy designed to minimize pressure on the players.

Charlie walks over to his sister, who is wheeling herself toward him. As she moves forward, she accidentally brushes against a player's leg while he's talking to another player.

"Oh, I'm really sorry I bumped into you. I didn't mean to. Are you okay?" Katie quickly apologizes, stopping to look at the young man. She knows it was just a light touch since she had been moving slowly.

But the young man glares at her angrily. "Are you blind? Can't you see where you're going?"

6

"I've said I'm sorry; it was just a small bump. Why are you so upset?" Katie responds firmly, beginning to wheel herself away.

But he steps in front of her, deliberately blocking her path with a mocking smirk on his face.

A young man behind him tugs on his shirt. "Come on, Jake. Let's go. Don't cause any trouble." He steps in front of Katie, gently steering Jake aside to clear her way.

Just then, Charlie catches up to his sister. He faces the young man and gives a nod, a quiet gesture of thanks.

Half an hour later, all participants have performed, and the judges are finalizing the scores. Then, the announcement begins. Katie and Krystal are both anxiously watching the results.

"The second runner-up is Jake Gibson from Paramount High, with 40 hits and 7 misses. He will receive a two-hundred-dollar scholarship."

The young man who Katie bumped into, steps onto the stage, raising his hand to the crowd with a cheer.

"The first runner-up is Charlie Santos from Willow Grove High, with a score of 42 hits and 4 misses. He will receive a five-hundred-dollar scholarship."

Charlie looks stunned. "Is that... me?" he murmurs to his sister. Katie gives him an encouraging push. "Go on,

Charlie! You did amazing. I'm so proud to be your sister!"

Charlie heads up to the stage, still in disbelief.

"And the first-place winner is Brandon Walker from Einstein High, with 45 hits and 3 misses. He will receive a one-thousand-dollar scholarship."

The young man who had pulled Jake back earlier strides onto the stage, pointing to the ceiling with a modest smile.

Katie turns to Krystal. "I know Brandon is way better than most players and totally deserved to win. But I'm surprised Charlie came in second."

Krystal smiles. "Well, Brandon is a senior, and isn't Charlie just a sophomore? He's got plenty of room to grow."

After the award ceremony, as everyone heads out to clear the gym, Charlie proudly shows Katie his award check.

"Sis, you can use this for your college fund," he says earnestly.

Katie chuckles. "No way, Charlie. This money is yours. Besides, I'm going to win the debate final against Einstein, and that prize is even bigger." She pats him on the arm with her right hand while using her left to propel her wheelchair forward, keeping pace with him as they head out together.

Charlie grins, holding up the check. "Then I'll get something for Mom — something she's really wanted. She's been working so hard for us."

Just then, a guy sneaks up behind them and makes a swift grab for the check. Under normal circumstances, the move might have succeeded with the element of surprise. But Charlie, who is visually impaired, relies on his "*Eyes of an Angel*" device to communicate his surroundings to him. Sensing the movement from behind, he quickly pulls his right hand in, clutching the check tightly, and pivots to face the would-be thief.

"Jake, why are you trying to snatch Charlie's award check?" Katie shouts, her voice ringing out across the hallway.

After failing to snatch Charlie's check and being called out by Katie, Jake feels a mix of embarrassment and anger. Stepping closer to Charlie, he sneers, "You're pretty quick, Charlie boy. How about a one-on-one? I'll prove I'm the better player and the one who really deserves that second-place award."

"No. I'm not into contact sports. I'm not playing with you." Charlie shakes his head, slipping the award check into his pocket. He gently touches Katie's shoulder and starts to walk away. He is not good with words but his silence says more than words ever could.

But Jake isn't ready to let him off that easy. "Coward, Charlie! You make Willow Grove ashamed!" He steps in front of Charlie, fists clenched, blocking his path.

"Actually, Willow Grove is proud of him," Katie cuts in. "Charlie placed second in the shootout. You came in third. That's forever in the record books. He's better than you, Jake, and you can't change that." Being the lead in a debating team, her voice is sharp and direct.

Jake's face darkens, his cheeks flushing with anger. He lunges forward and shoves Katie's wheelchair hard enough that it nearly tips over. Just then, a bystander catches it from the side, steadying her. "Hey, Jake, chill out! You almost hurt her!" he says.

"Back off, Brandon. This is between me and Charlie." Jake squares up, taking a boxer's stance, his eyes locked on Charlie.

Brandon makes a move to step between the two, but Krystal gently pulls him back. "Hold on, Brandon. I want to see how Charlie handles this. Step in only if things get out of hand."

At six-foot-five, Jake towers over the rest of the players in the tournament. He stands three inches taller than

Brandon and a full nine inches above Charlie. Charlie, facing him now, looks like David before Goliath.

But Charlie remains unwavering. Stepping behind Katie, he firmly grips the wheelchair handles. "We need to go. Now, if you'd excuse us," he says calmly, beginning to wheel Katie past the towering Jake.

"Oh, no, you don't." Jake lunges forward and shoves the wheelchair again, attempting to tip it over.

A crowd of bystanders watches, but no one steps in to intervene.

Charlie reacts instantly, releasing one hand from the wheelchair to grab Jake's wrist in a strong, unyielding grip. Jake feels the strength in Charlie's hold and instinctively steps back, then swings his free fist toward Charlie's face. But Charlie sidesteps, tilting his head just enough for the punch to sail harmlessly past. In the same motion, he lets go of Jake's wrist, resuming his calm stance.

The onlookers are stunned by Charlie's quick, precise response to Jake's aggression — everyone except Katie. Smiling to herself, she thinks, *All that hard work and practice with Uncle Jordan is paying off.*

Krystal's eyes widen in shock. "Charlie has vision problems, yet he can handle someone like Jake?" She turns to Brandon, waiting for his reaction.

Brandon nods thoughtfully. "It's possible. Charlie's probably been training himself to handle bullies for a while. Jake's bigger, so he's underestimating Charlie — especially with those funny-looking goggles."

With years of MMA training himself, he shares his observations with Krystal. "I noticed he shifts his right hip, preparing to kick, but he steps back right away. He doesn't want to hurt Jake. I admire that; he's staying so composed, not letting any of this shake him."

While Jake is standing there rubbing his wrist, Charlie speaks calmly. "Can I take my sister now, please? We can talk later, but this isn't the time."

Having felt the surprising strength in Charlie's grip, Jake realizes there's more to him than he first thought. Without a word, he steps aside, letting them pass.

A middle-aged man and his attractive wife watch the event unfold from a distance. As they see Charlie and Katie pass by Jake, they exchange a glance and nod with a knowing smile.

~ ~ ~ ~ ~

Chapter 2

When Courage Meets Challenge

After Katie and Charlie arrive home, their mother, Maria, greets them warmly.

"You must be tired after the competition, Charlie. Come and have some enchiladas," she says, gesturing for him to sit down. She doesn't ask how he did in the contest, simply exchanging a glance with Katie, assuming he wouldn't place very high. Charlie is still wearing his goggles.

But before Katie can say anything, Charlie steps forward and gives his mom a warm hug. "You'll never guess how I did, Mom, I came in second!" he exclaims, proudly holding up his award check for Maria to see.

"What? You came in second?" Maria is stunned. "How is that possible? You can't see like they do! You aimed and hit all your targets?" She glances at the check and stutters. "Five hundred dollars?" She exclaims in disbelief.

"Yes, Mom," Katie wheels over to the table, smiling. "You should've seen him — he runs and shoots like a pro! Better than most of the players here today. I was right there!"

The Santos family sits down, savoring the enchiladas.

"I got a call from your grandma this morning," Maria says to her children, her voice trembling slightly. "Grandpa fell yesterday and broke his right hip. He's bedridden now and can barely move. Grandma has to take care of everything for him." Her eyes glisten with tears. "I need to go see him. I'm taking a bus to Phoenix tonight."

"Oh no!" Katie and Charlie exclaim in unison, their faces falling.

"Mom," Charlie says, reaching for his checkbook, "I'd like to give my award to Grandma to help with medical expenses. She could use the money."

Maria's face softens into a smile. "You're such a good boy, Charlie. But it's your award — you should keep at least part of it. Set aside two hundred dollars for you and your sister."

Later that evening, after watching their mom depart at the bus stop, Katie and Charlie decide to grab a bite at a nearby pizza joint, to enjoy this Saturday night. The bus stop, located near Paramount High, sits in a rough neighborhood. Yet it's still a popular spot where students gather at night.

Charlie wheels Katie into the restaurant, and she quickly spots a few Paramount students laughing and drinking beer. One of them locks eyes with Charlie, staring intently. Sensing trouble, Katie touches her brother's arm and whispers, "Let's not stay. Let's just go."

But before Charlie can turn around, the guy who was staring steps in front of the doorway, blocking their exit.

"So, you're the guy from Willow Grove who beat Paramount, huh?" he says, standing in Charlie's way with his arms crossed. A couple of others step up beside him, each with a mocking smile.

Katie immediately pulls out her phone and dials 9-1-1, but she knows that in this neighborhood, especially on a Saturday night, the police might not arrive quickly.

The guy in front of Charlie laughs. "Cops take at least ten minutes to get here — if they even bother," he sneers, stepping closer. "By then, it'll be over." He starts rubbing his fists.

Charlie just stands still, saying nothing. He remembers Uncle Jordan's advice: during a confrontation, stay silent and wait. Don't be the first to move. He knows a fight is inevitable, but he wants to buy time for the police to arrive.

Impatient, the guy scoffs. "What's with the stupid goggles? Both of you!" He turns to Katie and reaches out his hand. "Let me take those off. Bet you're hiding your face behind them for a reason." He steps forward, attempting to grab Katie's goggles.

Charlie swiftly and forcefully flicks his right wrist, deflecting the guy's hand, and steps protectively in front of Katie. "Leave my sister alone!" he shouts firmly.

The guy feels as if his hand was struck by a baseball bat. He recoils but quickly recovers, anger flaring. He throws a quick left jab toward Charlie's face, aiming to follow up with a right hook to the jaw.

But Charlie is quicker. His right fist shoots up, deflecting the jab, then follows through to land a solid hit to the guy's face. Despite being outweighed by at least thirty pounds, the punch is powerful enough to send the guy stumbling back several steps, kicking over a chair, and finally caught by one of his friends.

"Are you okay, Brock?" his friend asks, but before he can respond, another guy charges at Charlie, fists raised and swinging.

Katie shouts, "Watch out!" just as Charlie pivots, delivering a powerful roundhouse kick to the guy's chest. He's sent flying back nearly seven feet, knocking over another chair, hitting the ground dazed and barely conscious.

The bystanders fall silent, stunned. No one can believe he's taken down two much bigger opponents with just two moves. No one dares to step forward.

Charlie stands still, one hand on Katie's shoulder and the other on the wheelchair handle, silently assessing the scene.

Brock struggles to help his friend to his feet, unsure of his next move. Then, the wail of a siren pierces the air. The gang quickly scatters, disappearing into the distance.

The old man behind the counter sighs, turning back to his pizza oven to retrieve a couple of pizzas. He seems to be the owner of the pizzeria, and it's clear he's seen scenes like this unfold countless times before.

Just then, a pair of police officers — a man and a woman — enter. The policeman scans the room and asks, "What's going on here?"

"A fight almost broke out, but those guys are gone now," the owner replies calmly.

The policewoman notices two chairs overturned and spots a girl in a wheelchair by the door, holding her phone and smiling. Beside her stands a young man, protectively close, both of them wearing thick goggles.

The policewoman walks up to the girl and introduces herself. "I'm Officer Mandy. Are you the one who called? Could you tell me what happened? We need to file a report for all calls."

"Yes, that was me," Katie replies. "My name is Katie Santos. My brother, Charlie, and I came in to grab a bite, but we were harassed by a few young men. They seemed a little too tipsy and started mocking us. I sensed things might escalate, so I called. They didn't want any trouble, so they took off quickly." Katie, clear and composed from her time on the debate team, explains the situation efficiently.

The policeman steps forward. "I'm Officer Brody. Katie, did you see any fighting break out? I noticed a couple of chairs knocked over."

The pizzeria owner cuts in. "Those chairs were already down before they arrived. A few kids were messing around earlier and knocked them over. I just hadn't had the chance to straighten up with so many customers coming in."

Katie nods at him from behind the officers and flashes a quick grin.

Not entirely convinced but seeing no other signs of violence, Officer Brody decides to close the case and exits with Officer Mandy. Outside, he remarks, "In my experience, there was definitely a fight in there, but it ended quickly, maybe just a few blows. Whoever stepped in must be very skilled. Who could that person be?"

Officer Mandy, more perceptive, considers the situation. "Katie was smiling and standing close to that young man, Charlie — he seemed like her protector. I'd bet he's the one who handled it, but he looks so young."

Officer Brody nods in agreement. "If someone has been training for a long time, they can be very skilled, regardless of their age. But what puzzles me is Charlie wearing those thick goggles — it usually points to a vision problem. How does someone with eyesight issues manage to fight so well?"

"True," she replies, starting the car. "Either way, we should be glad it hasn't escalated into more violence."

Back inside, Katie turns to the pizzeria owner. "Thanks, Uncle Leo," she says. "If I'd mentioned a fight, it would've been a headache trying to explain how it ended so fast." She glances proudly at Charlie, who's been quiet the whole time.

"These kids come around looking for trouble all the time," Leo replies with a smile. "It's refreshing to see

Charlie handle them so smoothly. I can tell Jordan's training has really paid off!" He hands Katie several slices of freshly baked pepperoni pizza. "Here, a few slices on the house for both of you."

As they sit down and start enjoying their pizza, Charlie leans over and whispers to Katie, "Is that guy in the corner Jake Gibson?"

Katie nods. "Yep, that's him," she whispers back. "This place is a popular hangout for Paramount High kids. He might know Brock — and could've even put him up to harass us."

But Jake just sits there quietly, biting his slice of pizza.

Charlie frowns. "But he's keeping to himself, not even joining his friends. What's he up to?" he wonders aloud.

— ✦ —

After they arrive home, Katie picks up her debate materials and starts reviewing for the upcoming competition against Einstein High. Meanwhile, Charlie takes a shower, takes off his goggles and then lies in bed, recalling the events of the day.

He remembers stepping onto the stage and standing next to Jake, feeling Jake's disgusted gaze fixed on him.

He recalls how Jake tried to snatch his check away and the moment when he felt Jake attempting to tip over Katie's wheelchair.

In his mind, he hears Uncle Jordan's voice: "Charlie, you're going to protect your mother and sister. You are the man of the family."

His thoughts drift back to ten years ago, to the first time he wore the "Eyes of an Angel" goggles invented by Uncle Fraser. Those goggles allowed him to navigate independently, but at that young age, he struggled to adapt to them.

When he started school, many students mocked and teased him — except Amanda. One grade ahead of him, she was a compassionate girl who often defended him. Though she could only do so much, her kindness made a difference.

He remembered that day when a few older students physically bullied him. Amanda reported it to the teachers and pulled him away, then, since she lived nearby, she walked him home.

That evening, Auntie Sarah and Uncle Jordan were visiting. When they saw him limping in with a bruised face, they were stunned. Naturally quiet, he stayed silent about what happened, so Amanda explained how he had been bullied.

He vividly recalls Uncle Jordan taking his hand, standing up, and saying firmly, "Charlie, you can't let yourself be treated this way. I'm going to teach you how to protect yourself."

Sarah interjected, "You're teaching him to fight? How can he? He can't see like the other kids!"

"No, not fighting, Sarah," Jordan replied calmly. "I'll teach him how to defend himself."

"But...can I? I can barely see them," He stammered, his voice uncertain.

Amanda chimed in encouragingly, "You're doing fine in school, Charlie. And you move around pretty well."

"You definitely can, Charlie," Jordan added with a reassuring smile. "If she believes in you, you should believe in yourself too."

Sarah joined in with a playful smile, noticing the special bond between him and Amanda. "Yes, you'll stand up, Charlie! You've got to look out for her in the years to come!"

Jordan then turned to him seriously and said, "Never start a fight, but be ready if it comes to you. You'll need to build your strength. I'll set up a training program and show you a few basic moves. The key is practice — again and again."

He recalls from that day forward, he spent countless hours each night learning and practicing. The training boosted his confidence, and he discovered that when he carried himself with determination and assertiveness, most bullies tended to back off.

His thoughts drift back to that evening in the pizzeria. *"If Amanda's there, and she only sees..."* A quiet smile crosses his face as he closes his eyes, savoring the memory.

~ ~ ~ ~ ~

Chapter 3
Cracks in Perfect Glass

Come Sunday morning.

After church, Katie and Charlie head to an upscale shopping mall to find a present for their mom. After a couple of hours of browsing, they settle on a coat. They then stop at a coffee shop to sit down and rest.

As they enter, Katie spots Krystal and Brandon chatting in a corner. She wheels herself over to say hello while Charlie waits in line to order their drinks.

Since ninth grade, Krystal and Brandon have been inseparable. Both tall, attractive, and from affluent families, they complement each other well: She, being in the debate team, is an excellent communicator. He, being in the basketball team, excels in all kinds of sports. Together, they truly seem like a match made in heaven.

"Seems like we're always bumping into you," Katie says, smiling at Krystal before turning to Brandon. "And you too!"

"Oh, Katie, please join us!" Brandon says, quickly pulling out a chair to make room for her wheelchair.

Katie wheels in and waves to Charlie, who's just picked up two coffees at the counter. Noticing her, he heads over.

"Hey, have you two met my brother? This is Charlie," Katie says, introducing him. "And Charlie, this is my good friends Krystal and Brandon — from Einstein High. Brandon won the shootout contest yesterday!"

"Hi, Krystal. Hi, Brandon," Charlie says, nodding with a friendly smile. "I saw you play yesterday — you really earned that win."

Charlie's words are a bit clumsy, but his admiration is genuine.

"I got a little lucky," Brandon replies modestly. "You're doing pretty well yourself, Charlie."

Katie glances over at Krystal, who's unusually quiet, her gaze distant and her eyes slightly wet. Concerned, Katie leans toward her. "Krystal, you seem off today. Do you want to talk about it?"

Krystal remains silent, looking down. Brandon catches Katie's eye and gives a slight shake of his head, signaling her to tread carefully.

Katie quickly senses the need for privacy. She picks up her cup. "Oh, I just remembered we still need to pick up groceries. We'd better get going." Catching the hint, Charlie hands his cup to Katie, steps behind her wheelchair, and they head out.

As they leave the coffee shop, Krystal's tears spill over. "I don't know what to do, Brandon," she says, her voice breaking.

Brandon gently takes her hand, offering a reassuring squeeze. "We can only wait and see, Kris. I trust that God will guide us."

— ✦ —

Outside, Katie is sharing her thoughts with Charlie.

"What's going on with Krystal? She was so cheerful yesterday at the shootout — she even mentioned you. But today, it's like she's a different person. I hope it's nothing serious."

Charlie answers thoughtfully. "When we came in, I heard her mention something about her mom." Though he can't see, his specialized 'Eyes of an Angel' goggles capture, filter, and amplify sounds, allowing him to pick up details most people miss.

"Her mom?" Katie recalls meeting her last year. "I remember her picking Krystal up after the debate. She's

26

beautiful, like Krystal, and so well-mannered. What could be wrong?"

Charlie hesitates before whispering, "I also overheard words like 'cheating' and 'divorce.' I hope I misheard."

Katie's heart sinks. She knows her brother wouldn't say something like that unless he was pretty sure. Growing up in a divorced family herself, she understands all too well what it's like to live with just one parent. But at least she's had her brother to lean on—they've always looked out for each other. Krystal, though, is an only child. A deep worry settles over Katie for her friend.

— ✦ —

Inside Krystal's luxurious home, a distinguished middle-aged man sits across from an attractive woman. The room is silent.

"Chelsea, I believe this is the only solution," he finally speaks, his voice soft but resolute.

Chelsea's eyes glisten with unshed tears as she replies, her voice barely above a whisper, "If it has to be this way, then so be it. But on one condition, Jon," Her tone strengthens. "Krystal will stay with me."

Jon's expression softens, though emotion lingers in his words. "Krystal is sixteen now. Shouldn't we let her decide? When she's calmed down and comes back, we need to talk to her."

Chelsea glances away, her voice filled with concern. "I'm worried about her. This morning, when she overheard us, she stormed out in tears. I've never seen her react like that. She's not answering her phone." She sighs, the weight of her worry apparent.

"Try not to worry too much, Chelsea. She's probably with Brandon. He's a good kid; he'll look after her." Jon tries to reassure her. "Let's give her some time to work through this. I'll reach out to Brandon later."

— ✦ —

After having coffee, Krystal isn't ready to go home, so Brandon takes her to his place to rest. However, with his siblings around, they decide to head to a nearby park and sit on a bench. Nearby, a man is playing tennis with his young son, while a woman chats with her daughter, both standing and watching as they play.

"What exactly happened?" Brandon asks gently. "Sometimes things aren't what they seem."

Krystal shakes her head, her voice heavy with emotion. "I wish that were true, but I don't think so." Tears begin to fill her eyes. "When I got home last night, neither of my parents were there. I don't know when they came back, but this morning I heard them arguing," she recalls.

Brandon stays quiet, his gaze soft, encouraging her to continue.

"I overheard Dad mention a video… of Mom kissing some man in our driveway," Krystal whispers, her voice trembling. "And then Mom said something about Dad spending too much time with Samantha. She's one of his major clients at the bank. He talks about her sometimes."

"They were getting louder and louder, and then I heard them mention divorce," Krystal continues, her voice trembling. "That's when I opened the door. I've never seen them look at each other with such anger, such hostility. They weren't the parents I've always known." She breaks down, sobbing onto Brandon's shoulder.

Just then, a tennis ball flies toward Krystal's head, but Brandon swiftly catches it before it makes contact.

A young boy runs over, out of breath, and says, "Sorry," holding out his hand for the ball.

Brandon hands it to him with a kind smile. "You're doing great out there with your dad. How old are you?"

"I'm almost seven," the boy replies proudly, before turning to Krystal. "Why are you making your sister cry?" he asks innocently.

Krystal looks up, trying to smile through her tears. "Oh no, he didn't make me cry," she reassures him softly. "He's just trying to help me feel better. What's your name?"

"Daniel," the boy answers. "What are your names?"

"I'm Krystal, and this is Brandon. It's nice to meet you, Daniel," Krystal says with a gentle smile.

As Daniel walks back to his game, Krystal watches him fondly. "He's so sweet. I wish I had a little brother like that." Her expression softens for a moment, but soon the weight of the morning's events clouds her face, and her voice grows heavier with the burden of her thoughts. Seeking a small bit of comfort, she leans into Brandon.

A woman watching the tennis game turns and glances at Krystal, her gaze lingering on Daniel as he spoke to the pair. "Is that girl from your school, Tiff?" she asks her daughter.

"Yes, she is, Mom," Tiffany replies thoughtfully. "She's a few grades ahead of me. I think she's a senior, but I can't remember her name. I always see her with Brandon."

"You know her friend's name but not hers?" her mom teases with a playful smile.

"Mom, Brandon's Caitlin's brother, and the captain of our basketball team! Tons of girls like him, but he only ever seems to pay attention to her," Tiffany said, a hint of irritation creeping into her voice. "And seriously, Mom, I'm only nine!"

Back on the bench, with Krystal resting her head on his shoulder, Brandon searches for words to comfort her but comes up short. Suddenly, his phone rings.

"Hey Brandon, where are you?" his mother's voice sounds on the other end.

"I'm at the park with Krystal. What's up, Mom?" he asks.

"Brett called. He's running a high fever, and your dad and I won't be home until late tonight. Can you take him to the ER? Call us when you know more," she says, her tone laced with concern.

Brett is Brandon's 12-year-old brother. He also has a 9-year-old sister.

Brandon turns to Krystal. "Brett's sick, and I need to take him to the hospital. Do you want to come with me or should I take you home first?" His voice is sincere. "You know, sooner or later you'll need to talk to your parents. But remember, I'm always here for you."

"I want to stay with you, Brandon," Krystal replies softly. "I'm not ready to face my parents yet."

Brandon rushes home, grabs his brother, and drives to the hospital with Krystal sitting quietly beside him. When they arrive at the ER, he tells her to stay in the car while he checks Brett in.

As Krystal waits, her thoughts begin to wander. She drifts back to when she was eight, sitting with her mother as she read her the story of how Cinderella met Prince Charming. Krystal had asked, "Mom, how did you meet Dad?"

Her mother hesitated for a moment, then smiled softly. "Before I met your dad, I was a singer at some small casinos in Las Vegas. One night, your dad came to a show with a few friends, and he noticed me. It didn't take long before we fell for each other."

"You were a singer, Mom? No wonder you sing so beautifully," she had asked innocently. "Mom, you're so pretty. Did anyone besides Dad ever try to get to know you?"

She still vividly remembers her mother's silent reaction — how her cheeks flushed lightly and a soft smile played on her lips. Now, at sixteen, Krystal understands what that look really meant.

Her thoughts wander to her tenth birthday. After she blew out the candles, her dad smiled and asked, "What's your wish, sweetie?"

Without hesitation, she had replied, "I wish for a baby brother or sister."

She instantly noticed the change in her parents' expressions—their faces fell, and an awkward silence filled the room. After a moment, her mom quietly picked up the knife and said, "How about we cut the cake?"

"Why did they seem upset when I wished for a younger sibling?" Krystal wondered to herself. "Mom and Dad can definitely afford to have another child, so why aren't they planning to?" The question lingered in her mind.

Just then, Brandon came out of the hospital.

"The doctor said Brett has some kind of stomach infection," he explained. "They treated him, but he needs to stay overnight for observation." He looked at her with concern. "Your dad called me a little while ago. They're worried about you. I should take you home now."

He gave her a warm, comforting hug. "I'll wait outside by the driveway for a while. If you need to get out or talk, I'll be right there."

— ✦ —

Back at Krystal's house, Jon speaks to Chelsea, "I just talked to Brandon. He's bringing Krystal back soon."

"What are we going to tell her?" Chelsea asks, her voice calmer now, but her thoughts still troubled. "She heard us yelling about divorce. Is that really the only option for us? I love you, Jon."

"No, Chelsea, you don't," Jon replies softly, though emotion tightens his voice. "You say you love me because I can give you and Krystal a stable family. But your heart still belongs to Travis."

Chelsea falls silent, tears welling up and streaming down her cheeks as Jon continues, "All these years, I've wanted us to have another child, but you've refused. You're afraid that having a child with me will bind you to a life you don't want."

"But is Krystal enough? I see you love her as much as I do," Chelsea responds with a trembling voice.

"Yes, I love her … but she's not my child…" Hesitantly as Jon speaks, Krystal walks in.

~ ~ ~ ~ ~

Chapter 4
The Shelter – and Beyond

Katie and Charlie are home after dinner. While Charlie heads to the backyard to practice his moves, Katie sits in the quiet room, staring at the debate materials spread out in front of her, unable to focus.

Krystal is both a good friend and a formidable opponent. But how can she perform well in the debate competition, knowing her parents are going through a divorce? Katie cares a lot for her, but deep down, she's also jealous. Krystal has everything Katie doesn't — beauty, wealth, two loving parents, and even a boyfriend every girl admires.

Deep down, Katie feels that the only way to balance her conflicted feelings is to win the debate against Krystal fair and square. Now given everything Krystal is facing, Katie is sure she has an advantage. But what if Krystal decides to withdraw?

Suddenly, a wave of shame hits her. *Why am I even thinking about winning? She's my friend, and she's going through such a difficult time. She needs support, not competition.*

Katie picks up her phone and dials. Surprisingly, Brandon picks up the call.

"Katie, thanks for calling. Krystal is with me right now," he says, his voice full of concern. "She's… really lost. She can't stay at home. Do you think I could bring her over to stay with you for a few nights?" He hesitates briefly, then adds, "She doesn't have many close friends at school that she trusts. I know you're her best friend, and she could really use some company."

Hearing Brandon's words, Katie feels a pang of emotion as her eyes start to well up. *She thinks of me as her best friend, and I've been jealous of her? That's not who I am,* she reflects.

"Absolutely, Brandon," she replies, her voice filled with warmth. "Bring her over. I'll make sure she feels welcome, and we'll have plenty of time to talk."

Charlie is in the backyard when he hears footsteps approaching the front door. He opens the side gate and recognizes Brandon and Krystal. "Hey, Brandon, Krystal. You're here to see my sister? It's pretty late."

"Yes, is she home?" Krystal replies softly, her voice subdued. "Charlie, I need to stay here for a few days… if that's okay."

Before Charlie can respond, Katie appears at the doorway. "Come on in, both of you," she says warmly.

36

Upon seeing her, Krystal steps forward and bends down to embrace her, tears streaming down her cheeks. "Thank you for letting me stay. I just… I don't know what to do," she says, her voice trembling.

"Krystal, I know exactly how you feel," Katie says, wrapping her arms around Krystal's shoulders. "I'm so glad you came over. We're best friends, remember?" she adds warmly, her voice full of sincerity.

Once they're all inside, Katie gestures toward her mom's room. "You can sleep in my mom's bed; she's away for a week or so." Leading Krystal to the room, she adds, "Mom and I share this room, and Charlie has the other one. Unpack, and then we can talk."

Meanwhile, Brandon and Charlie are chatting in the living room.

"You and your sister didn't seem surprised when I brought Krystal over," Brandon observes.

"When we saw her at the coffee shop this morning, she didn't look happy. We figured something was up," Charlie replies.

Brandon glances toward the bedroom door. "Let her share whatever's going on with your sister. I'd better get going." He stands, pausing for a moment to look at Charlie before asking, "Charlie, you played so well in the tournament. Why haven't I seen you on your school's team? With you, Willow Grove could probably be among the top three in the county."

Charlie hesitates, then replies, "I'm not into contact sports. Confronting people face-to-face isn't my strength." He shifts slightly before adding, "Plus, I'm legally blind and have to rely on special goggles. I can't really play in team settings." He feels a bit vulnerable but trusts Brandon, knowing he's a close friend of his sister's best friend.

"Legally blind? And you can play basketball?" The words almost slip out, but Brandon catches himself, sensing it's best not to pry further out of respect.

"Alright, I'll come by tomorrow morning to pick her up for school. Good night," he says as he steps out the door.

— ✦ —

In Katie's room, Krystal opens up about what she overheard that day.

"What should I do, Katie? I can't believe both my parents are having affairs," she says, her voice breaking as tears spill over. "And tonight, when I got home, I heard my dad say that I'm not his daughter. How am I supposed to deal with that?"

"Take a breath, Krystal," Katie replies gently. "Sometimes what we overhear isn't the full story. Have you spoken to your parents and asked them to explain what they meant?"

"No… maybe I should," Krystal says, calming slightly. "But I was in shock this morning, and when I opened the door, they just stared at each other and ignored me. It feels like what I heard has to be true."

"And you're sure you heard your dad say you're not his daughter? Are you positive?" Katie asks gently, though she knows Krystal, as the debate team leader, rarely misinterprets what she hears.

"Yes," Krystal replies, her voice steady but strained. "That's what I heard when I walked in tonight. I thought things would have calmed down enough for us to talk, but then I heard Dad mention a name — Travis. Then he said I wasn't his child." She pauses, gathering herself. "I remember Mom once told me she used to have a boyfriend before she met my Dad."

Krystal's gaze drops as she adds softly, "I looked at my mom… and she didn't deny it. She just kept silent and looked… hurt."

Katie pauses thoughtfully. "But do you remember if Auntie kept seeing this Travis even after she married Uncle?"

"Not that I know of," Krystal replies, her brow furrowing as she thinks. "But I've noticed that Dad's been talking to her less and less over the past few years." She adds, "I spend most of my time with Mom, and sometimes I wouldn't see Dad for days."

"Communication is the foundation of any loving relationship," Katie says with a hint of sadness. "It sounds like this has been brewing for a while, and now… it's finally come to a boiling point."

Both girls sit in silence. Katie knows all too well what it's like to grow up in a broken family, but she struggles to find the right words to comfort Krystal.

Just then, a text message comes through.

"It's my mom," Krystal says, glancing at her phone. "She says we should all calm down and that she'll talk to me in a day or so."

"Then let's try to get some rest," Katie says, feeling a bit more relieved. "It's been a long day, and we have school tomorrow."

After their nighttime routines, the girls get ready for bed. Krystal watches as Katie wheels herself over to her bed, grabs a cane, and smoothly transfers herself onto it.

Unable to hold back her curiosity, she asks, "Katie, it's amazing to see you move so well. Didn't you mention you had cerebral palsy as a kid? And now you've recovered?"

"Yes, Krystal," Katie says, her voice filled with gratitude. "It's all thanks to Uncle Fraser. He invented these special goggles to help me train my brain to control my body." She takes off the goggles and places them on the nightstand.

Krystal stares at her, stunned into silence.

"What? Why are you looking at me like that?" Katie asks, touching her face, confused. "I'm pretty sure I washed my face."

"You... you look so pretty!" Krystal finally blurts out. "I didn't even notice when you had those big, thick goggles on."

"Me? Pretty? Come on," Katie responds with a playful smirk. "And that's coming from the beauty queen of Einstein?"

"No, I mean it — you really are charming, without makeup or anything," Krystal sighs, then adds, "Oh, and you mentioned the goggles helped you train your brain to control your body? Is that even possible? How does it work?"

"I don't know much about the science behind it, Krystal," Katie admits with a smile. "All I know is that the goggles capture other people's movements and somehow send that information to my brain. Then my brain learns to give the same commands to my body to mimic the movement."

Her expression softens as she remembers the day Fraser fitted her with the helmet and goggles, patiently guiding her through each step.

"But … Charlie wears the same type of goggles as you," Krystal says, unable to hold back her curiosity. "Didn't you mention he's visually impaired?"

"He is," Katie nods. "Uncle Fraser designed Charlie's goggles to work a bit like a car's autopilot. They give him signals about his surroundings so he can navigate independently," she adds, gratitude evident in her voice.

"And Charlie is shooting baskets so well! It's unbelievable!" Krystal exclaims, clearly captivated by Katie's story and momentarily distracted from her own troubles.

"He's an incredibly hardworking kid," Katie says with pride. "It's amazing what he's been able to accomplish."

Thinking back to the time she watched Charlie skillfully defend against Jake, Krystal nods in agreement. "Yeah, he really is something."

Meanwhile, Brandon is back home after visiting Brett in the hospital to make sure there is no complications. It's been a long day, and he's lying in bed, lost in thought.

"It's so kind of Katie to let Krystal stay with her for these few nights. She really needs a friend she can trust right now," he muses, recalling an image of Katie — a girl with thick, oversized goggles, smiling from her wheelchair.

He's only met Katie a handful of times at debate competitions and basketball games, and, being so focused on Krystal, he hadn't given her much thought. Yet he'd always been a little curious about this girl who, despite her physical challenges, communicates with such ease and confidence.

Tonight, however, he's struck by the warmth Katie showed to both him and Krystal in her home. "That's real friendship," he reflects, a growing sense of admiration stirring within him.

His mind drifts back to yesterday's shootout competition. "Katie's so assertive with Jake, never intimidated by his size — even from her wheelchair. How does she do it?" His curiosity deepens.

And then there's Charlie. He'd mentioned being legally blind, yet somehow possesses the awareness and skill to protect himself and his sister. "How is that even possible?" Brandon wonders aloud. "And what kind of goggles are they both wearing?"

Intrigued, he finds himself captivated by this remarkable pair of siblings.

Back in his room, Charlie is chatting with Amanda on the phone.

"Sorry, Charlie," Amanda says apologetically. "Yesterday was my dad's birthday, so our whole family went out to celebrate. But I heard you won second place! I wish I could have been there to cheer you on!"

"Family comes first, Amanda," Charlie replies sincerely. "But even though you weren't there, I felt your presence. It was like I knew you were watching me. Without that, I don't think I'd have made those shots."

"Oh, that's so sweet," Amanda says with a warm smile. "I've always believed in you. I still remember the day Uncle Jordan offered to train you — the determined look on your face was unforgettable."

"But without my mom, my sister, and you supporting me, I couldn't have done it. If it were just up to me, it would have felt pointless," he admits, finally expressing a truth he's held inside for so long. After a brief pause, he adds shyly, almost in a whisper, "I have to stand up. Auntie Sarah told me to look out for you in the years to come."

44

Amanda feels a swell of emotion, touched that Charlie remembers those words so vividly. Before she can respond, he continues.

"You three are the most important people in my life," he says with newfound courage.

They fall into a quiet moment, letting the sentiment linger. Finally, Charlie breaks the silence, smiling. "So... how about grabbing some pizza after school tomorrow to celebrate?"

"Is that a date?" Amanda laughs, her eyes turning bright. "Deal!"

~ ~ ~ ~ ~

Chapter 5
Two Emotions, One Courage

Jon and Chelsea stand in silence, looking at each other in their mansion's spacious living room. Finally, Jon speaks, breaking the stillness. "Krystal's going to Stanford in September. Let's wait until then," he says in a low, somber voice. "No matter what happens, I'll still take care of her college expenses."

Chelsea's voice trembles as she responds, her eyes filling with tears. "Is there really no other way? You love her as much as I do. How can she focus on her studies if she knows we're going through a divorce? It's so unfair to her."

Jon's face hardens, but a hint of emotion surfaces as he replies, "It's already been unfair to me, taking care of Travis's child all these years." He pauses, looking away to avoid Chelsea's gaze, his voice softening. "Now, finally, I have a chance to have my own child."

Chelsea stands there, speechless, feeling the weight of his words. She knows how deeply Jon has longed for a child of their own, and though she saw this coming, it still pierces her. She wonders if his desire for a child is the only reason he's pushing for this.

"Is it Samantha?" she asks, barely above a whisper. "She's a good woman. I wish you happiness." It's all she can bring herself to say.

— ✦ —

In the morning, Brandon arrives at Katie's house to pick up Krystal for school. As he waits, he notices her walking out with Katie and Charlie. He considers offering the siblings a ride, but hesitates when he notices Katie in her wheelchair, realizing he can't fit it in his car.

Katie quickly catches on to his hesitation and smiles. "You should head out—traffic can be slow on the way to Einstein," she says warmly, waving at Charlie. "We're going in a different direction and taking the bus is convenient for us. We're about to leave, too." Her words put Brandon at ease, sensing she understood his unspoken thought.

As Charlie and Katie settle onto the bus, Charlie is immediately greeted by a chorus of friends.

"Hey, Charlie! Willow Grove is so proud of you. It's the first time we've ever taken second place in the shootout!" says Jackson, a fellow basketball player, clapping him on the back.

Miguel gives him an approving nod. "Charlie, you almost beat Brandon! Nobody's ever come that close before," he says, patting Charlie's shoulder.

Jenny chimes in, her voice filled with admiration. "We were so worried when Jake started harassing you. He's huge — he could have easily overpowered you. How did you stand up to him like that?"

Charlie smiles, accepting their praise with quiet gratitude. But he doesn't respond, his gaze instead drifting toward the corner of the bus, where Amanda is sitting. She looks up, meeting his goggles with a bright smile that warms him more than any of the compliments.

— ✦ —

Krystal sits quietly in Brandon's car, looking noticeably more relaxed as he drives. Brandon keeps his focus on the road but occasionally glances over at her, sensing that silence is what she needs most right now. He knows that in moments like these, the best support he can offer is simply being there, ready to listen whenever she decides to speak. Besides, he feels reassured, trusting that Katie has comforted her enough to carry her through until she's ready to face her parents again.

"I feel a lot better now," Krystal finally says, breaking the silence. "Last night, we talked for hours, and it made me realize that Katie and Charlie have faced much bigger challenges than I have." She sighs. "They both have physical limitations, yet they live fuller lives than most people I know."

"They really are amazing," Brandon nods in agreement. "Their goggles might hint at what they've been through physically, but their attitude shows no limits."

Krystal smiles, a hint of admiration in her eyes. "It's something I look up to. Just a day ago, I felt like I had everything a girl could want, and then suddenly, it all seemed to disappear."

"Not everything," Brandon says gently, reaching over to take her hand. "You still have me, right here by your side."

Krystal leans against Brandon's shoulder, a mixture of tears and a faint smile in her eyes.

When they arrive at Einstein High, students glance their way. They're used to seeing Krystal's mom dropping her off, but today it's Brandon. So while no one is really surprised to see them together, they are taken aback by the tears in her eyes. Krystal has always been the one with a bright, cheerful smile, never letting sadness show.

"Morning, Krystal. Morning, Brandon," Alicia says as she walks past without stopping.

"Hey, Krystal. Hey, Brandon," Bonnie greets, continuing on her way.

Krystal gives a small nod and quietly heads toward her classroom. Since she started dating Brandon a few years ago, she's noticed her friends pulling back, distancing themselves out of quiet jealousy. And the boys? They admire her from afar, but they keep their distance too, knowing they can't compete with Brandon.

Usually, it doesn't bother her much — but today, it feels different. Today, it hurts.

During recess, Krystal bumps into April.

"Hey, Krystal. You seem a bit off today. Is something bothering you?" April asks gently. She's in the same AP Biology class and one of the few friends Krystal usually feels comfortable opening up to. But today, she is the last person Krystal wants to see.

Because she's Samantha's daughter.

"Oh, nothing much, just feeling a little under the weather," Krystal replies, forcing a smile. "Thanks for asking, April."

As April walks away, Krystal sinks onto a bench, lost in thought. *Maybe she doesn't know about her mom and*

Dad's affair. But even if she did... would she welcome it? She'd finally have a dad. But what about me?

Her mind drifts back to the day she visited her dad's bank. Jon and Samantha were discussing options for her deposit accounts in his office, while April sat outside on the couch, absorbed in her phone. Their parents' friendship had brought them together quickly as friends too.

But little did she know then — her dad and April's mom were more than just friends.

She doesn't know Samantha very well, having only seen her three or four times. All she knows is that Samantha has been a widow for some time, raising April on her own. April's father left them several rental properties—both commercial and residential — so they've been comfortably living off the rental income.

"She's soft-spoken, not aggressive, and definitely not as pretty as Mom. Why would Dad be interested in her?" Krystal wonders.

— ✦ —

"How am I going to tell her?" Chelsea sits alone on the couch, her mind a whirlwind of emotions. Jon had just left the house — probably to see Samantha.

51

"Why did I let Travis kiss me that night? Jon never checks the surveillance footage, so why did he look at it then? He must have known Travis was with me that night." Questions flood her mind.

She hadn't seen Travis since marrying Jon — until two years ago. They were celebrating their fifteenth anniversary at a bar-restaurant with Krystal when she suddenly recognized the guitarist on stage. Took a while before he looked down, and their eyes locking in an instant.

They kept their distance, neither embracing, shaking hands, nor exchanging a single word. Yet the look on his face and the expression in Chelsea's eyes spoke volumes, revealing a history Jon hadn't known before.

For the rest of the dinner, Jon and Chelsea remained unusually quiet, leaving Krystal puzzled about what was going on.

It was the first time Jon and Krystal had ever seen Travis.

Just as they were about to leave, Chelsea heard Travis speak into the microphone, introducing his next song.

"This next song is dedicated to the only woman I've ever loved. I don't know where she is right now," he said, glancing in her direction. "But wherever you are, I wish you all the best."

The haunting melody of '*I Will Always Love You*' filled the room, and a wave of unspoken memories crashed over Chelsea, leaving her breathless.

... We both know I'm not what you, you need

And I will always love you ...

As Travis's voice faded, Chelsea kept her gaze fixed forward, fighting the tears that welled in her eyes. She was unaware of her own expression but couldn't ignore Jon's silent stillness beside her — the way he sat motionless, his eyes carrying a profound sadness, a quiet mix of understanding and heartbreak.

Her hands trembled as she finally bit her lip and reached for her phone.

Krystal is having lunch with Brandon in the canteen when her phone buzzes. It's her mom calling.

"Hey, sweetie," Chelsea's voice is gentle, almost cautious. "Can you come home tonight? We need to talk. Your dad won't be home for a few days. We thought it might be better to speak with you separately first, then have a family conversation later."

Krystal pauses, the weight of her mother's words sinking in. "Sure, Mom. I'll come home tonight," she replies quietly, her voice calm but detached. She ends the call and sets her phone down, staring blankly at the table.

Without a word, Brandon reaches over and takes her hand in his, silently letting her know he's there.

— ✦ —

Right after school ends, Charlie meets Katie by the gate.

"Sis, I'm going with Amanda to grab some pizza. Want to join us?" he asks sincerely, his voice warm and inviting.

Katie smiles at his offer, her heart lightened by his thoughtfulness. She's glad to see him spending time with Amanda, and even more touched that he wanted her to come along.

"No, Charlie," she replies, her smile soft but genuine. "I need to head home and start preparing for the debate next month. You and Amanda have a great time."

With that, she gives him an encouraging nod before wheeling herself toward the bus stop, feeling a quiet pride in her little brother.

Willow Grove High isn't far from Paramount High, and the bus stop sits somewhere in between. It's not unusual for students from the two schools to cross paths there, but their rivalry often sparks tension. Conflicts occasionally break out, especially among those eager to prove their dominance.

As Katie waits in line for the bus, her heart skips a beat when she spots Brock — the young man from the pizzeria who had tried to harass her and Charlie that night. His eyes lock onto her, and a smirk spreads across his face when he notices her in the wheelchair. He starts moving toward her with slow, deliberate steps.

Katie's pulse quickens as she senses trouble brewing. Normally, in a situation like this, she would signal Charlie immediately — a precaution they had planned for moments like these. But this time, she hesitates.

"Charlie's with Amanda, having a good time. Should I really bother him?" The thought flashes through her mind. *"I can't rely on him forever. There are plenty of other students here. I'll see what he thinks he can do to me."*

She tightens her grip on the wheels of her chair, her eyes steady and determined, bracing herself for whatever might come next.

Brock steps closer, his smirk widening as he closes the distance between them. Katie notices he's alone this time, with none of his usual crew trailing behind.

"Well, well," Brock sneers, his voice dripping with mockery. "Where's your little brother, my fair lady?" He glances around, making sure Charlie isn't nearby.

55

Katie meets his gaze head-on, her goggles reflecting his image like a mirror. With a mocking smile, she replies, "He's not with me today. He has a life—unlike some people who seem to waste theirs causing trouble all day."

Her words slice through the air, sharp and steady, as she braces herself for what's to come.

Brock suddenly feels a twinge of discomfort, her unrelenting stare boring into him, unnervingly similar to Darth Vader's icy, penetrating gaze. For a moment, his confidence wavers, but he pushes forward, determined not to show weakness.

Stepping closer, he shouts, "Last time, you got lucky the cops showed up so fast. But this time, let's see who's gonna stop me!" His voice booms with forced bravado, deliberately ignoring the truth — that it was Charlie, not the police, who knocked him out last time.

As his anger flares, he lunges forward, his large hand reaching for Katie's goggles, intent on tearing them off.

Around them, a crowd of students gathers closer. Yet, not a single person steps forward to help. Their silence shows a mix of fear and indifference as the tension escalates.

~ ~ ~ ~ ~

Chapter 6
Same Resolve, Different Generations

Krystal sits across from Chelsea at the dining table, her expression calm but guarded. She had asked Brandon to wait in the driveway, unsure of how this conversation with her mom might unfold.

Chelsea takes a deep breath, her voice soft as she begins. "Do you remember the dinner we had two years ago at that bar-restaurant? The guitarist who sang on stage ... that was Travis, my ex-boyfriend. I hadn't seen him since I married your dad."

Krystal doesn't respond immediately as she listens. At that time, she was only fourteen. She didn't fully grasp the complexities of her parents' emotions, but she remembered being deeply moved by the raw emotion in Travis's voice as he sang that night.

Chelsea continues, her eyes gazing into her past. "Travis and I were in the same band before I went solo in Las Vegas. It was just a small group of four — nothing big or famous. We played in nightclubs, on cruises, and in small casinos. It wasn't glamorous, but it was ours."

She pauses, her shoulders sagging slightly. "Then, one day, our band leader was arrested on drug charges. He was imprisoned, and the band fell apart after that." Chelsea sighs, the weight of the memory pressing down on her.

Krystal leans back slightly, taking in her mother's words, the silence between them thick with unspoken emotions.

"Mom, you and Travis… why didn't you two get married? And why did you end up separating?" Krystal finally voices the questions that have lingered in her mind.

Chelsea's gaze softens as she begins. "We didn't have money, sweetie," she says gently. "Being in a traveling band was expensive, and when the band broke up, we had little savings left." She pauses, a faint glimmer of nostalgia in her eyes, then continues.

"Travis wanted to save enough so we could have a proper wedding, something special, and a secure future to start a family. We were in Las Vegas at the time, where most people settle for quick marriage registrations. But Travis didn't want that."

A bittersweet smile crosses her face as she adds, "He wanted it to mean something — something we could cherish forever."

Krystal studies her mother closely, sensing there's more to the story. "What happened, Mom? What did he do?"

Chelsea's shoulders sag under the weight of the memory. "When our band broke up, we struggled to find opportunities as a duo. I could still perform as a solo singer, but he couldn't. Maybe it was because I'm a woman, and people were more willing to give me a chance."

She sighs deeply, the pain evident in her voice.

"He couldn't handle being left behind. He tried to take the easy way out — he started gambling. This was Las Vegas, after all, and temptation was everywhere."

Her voice trails off, and the room falls silent as the truth settles between them, heavy and undeniable.

"So that's the reason you left him, Mom?" Krystal asks. She already has a sense of the consequences.

Chelsea shakes her head slightly, her voice dropping to a whisper. "No, not exactly," she says. "He took a loan from a loan shark, thinking he could win it back gambling. But he lost everything, and they came after him. He was beaten badly, and they warned him they'd break his arms — or worse — if he couldn't repay the debt."

Krystal's mouth falls open, but no words come out. The shock leaves her speechless.

Chelsea continues, her voice heavy with sadness. "During the time we were still performing as a band, there was a wealthy widow who always had her eye on him. So at that time he had no choice but to agree to marry her — to use her money to pay off the loan shark."

The room falls silent, the weight of Chelsea's words pressing down on both of them. Krystal's mind races, trying to process the heartbreak and betrayal woven into her mother's past.

As Brandon waits outside in the driveway, his phone buzzes with a text from Krystal:

"I'll stay home with Mom tonight. Drive carefully, and I'll see you tomorrow."

He exhales a sigh of relief, the tension in his shoulders easing. With a faint smile, he starts the car and drives off.

Later that evening, as Charlie walks into the house, he finds Katie in the kitchen. She greets him with a warm smile.

"How was your day with Amanda?" Katie asks, her tone light and teasing.

"It was nice," Charlie replies shyly, glancing away. "We walked and talked for a bit, and, uh, we accidentally passed by Uncle Leo's pizza place. I wanted to go somewhere else, but she really wanted pizza there."

Katie chuckles, her eyes sparkling with mischief. "Of course, you went along with her! Free pizza, plus Uncle Leo gets to tell her how heroic you were that night. Total win-win!" She grins, clearly enjoying her chance to tease him.

Charlie groans lightly. "Yes, he did tell her, and it was *so* embarrassing," he mutters. Then, after a moment, he adds softly, "But... it seems like she liked hearing the story."

Katie laughs again, her heartwarming at her brother's awkward charm. "Well, sounds like you're doing something right, Charlie."

Suddenly, Charlie notices Katie isn't wearing her goggles as she works in the kitchen.

"Sis, you're not wearing your goggles, and you can still work?" he asks curiously.

Katie pauses, hesitating for a moment before answering. "Oh, have I told you? I don't actually need my goggles anymore," she admits softly. "They've already done their job, training my brain to perform normal functions ninety-five percent of the time — except for my legs. The muscles there were damaged beyond recovery, so I still need the wheelchair."

She glances at him, her voice dropping slightly. "This is a secret I haven't told anyone, so please keep it that way, Charlie."

"Of course, I will. But ... why keep it a secret?" Charlie asks, his tone both curious and concerned.

Katie looks at him affectionately, a gentle smile on her face. "Because you still need to wear your goggles all the time. I just wanted to keep you company so people would treat us the same," she replies warmly.

Charlie's heart swells, understanding the quiet strength and care behind her words. "Thanks, sis," he is so moved by her gesture.

Katie nods. "By the way, Charlie, Krystal texted me to say she's staying home with her mom tonight. It sounds like they've reconciled. That's good news," she said with a small smile.

Later that night, after finishing her evening routine, Katie pauses in front of the mirror. She studies her reflection, aware that she isn't bad-looking but certainly doesn't consider herself on Krystal's level of beauty. She had always preferred to hide behind her goggles, letting her skills and abilities define her so people wouldn't focus on her appearance.

But Krystal's words from the night before lingered in her mind. Those were the words of a beauty queen, and she knew girls like Krystal didn't hand out compliments lightly—especially to other girls. For the first time, she began to wonder if there was truth in what Krystal had said.

Her thoughts drift back to the afternoon, to the tense encounter at the bus stop when Brock approached and tried to grab her goggles. She knew it would be pointless to resist physically, but Krystal's words echoed in her mind, sparking an idea. *"He wants to frighten me into submission, but I'm not going to let him,"* she had resolved.

Brock's hand grabbed Katie's goggles and ripped it off her face.

He was expecting to see a frightened, humiliated girl turning away, retreating in her wheelchair. He was ready to laugh.

But what he saw instead stunned him. Katie sat there calmly, meeting his gaze with a serene, inviting smile that lit up her face. The transformation was startling — her beauty, understated yet undeniable, caught him completely off guard. His heart skipped a beat as confusion overtook his smug expression.

He had seen pretty girls before—some aggressive, quick to fight back; others passive, shrinking away from confrontation.

But this girl in a wheelchair was different. Her calm confidence spoke louder than any words ever could.

Katie extended her hand, her voice composed and polite.

"Could you please return my goggles now?" she asked.

There was no fear in her tone—only quiet authority.

In that moment, she realized something powerful: a confident smile from a pretty girl could disarm even the most aggressive of men.

Still dumbfounded, Brock placed the goggles back into her hand without a word, watching in silence as Katie wheeled onto the bus with quiet dignity.

This wasn't how it usually went.

His world had always been simple—fight or flight, nothing in between. He fought. Others ran. That was the pattern.

But this girl broke it.

She didn't fight.
She didn't plead.

She didn't need to.

And she was in a wheelchair.

Somehow, that unsettled him more than anger ever had.

Back at home, Krystal breaks the heavy silence, her voice barely above a whisper. "Is Travis my real father? How did Dad find out?"

Deep down, she struggles with the revelation. The thought of being connected to a gambler, a man who married for money, stirs a mix of resentment and unease within her.

Chelsea hesitates, her gaze dropping to her hands before she finally looks up. "Yes, he is," she says softly. Her voice wavers as she takes a deep breath, gathering the strength to continue.

"My heart ached when I saw him beaten so badly," Chelsea begins, her words trembling. "But when he told me he was going to marry Melissa ... I didn't know how to feel. I was shocked, angry, and it all felt so unreal. He wasn't just leaving me—he was leaving *us*."

Tears well up in her eyes as she speaks. She dabs at her cheeks but doesn't stop, determined to tell Krystal the truth. "I hated him for what he did, but I also knew he thought it was the only way to fix the mess he'd made. I tried to move on, for both of us."

"Then I met your dad," Chelsea continues, her lips curling into a faint, bittersweet smile. "It didn't take long before he proposed to me. Given my situation at the time, I accepted. I thought marrying him would let me leave the past behind and start fresh."

Her voice falters slightly, and pauses before adding, "But then, Travis called. He wanted to see me ... just one last time. We met the night before my wedding."

She pauses, her gaze fixed on the floor, her eyes shadowed by the weight of memory. Krystal watches her, the raw emotion on her mother's face pulling tightly at her own heart.

"Why... what..." Krystal tries to ask, but the words tangle in her throat, unable to find their shape.

Still looking down, Chelsea whispers, her voice fragile. "He told me he and Melissa were moving to Paris. He wanted to say goodbye... to wish me a good life." Her voice trembles as she lifts her eyes to meet Krystal's, a lost and distant look in her gaze. "We were so emotional that night... and had one drink too many... more than we should have..."

Tears stream down both their faces, the air between them thick with sorrow and understanding. Chelsea wipes at her cheeks and whispers, "It's the one thing I regret most in my entire life."

Krystal doesn't say a word, her face frozen in a blank stare as she tries to process the confession. At sixteen, she can grasp her mother's emotions better than she wants to admit. Deep down, a part of her wonders: if Brandon were in Travis's place, would she have acted any differently? The answer makes her stomach churn.

After a long pause, Krystal takes a deep breath, her voice trembling. "Mom, did you and Dad still get married after that? Why did Dad say I'm not his daughter? Is that true?" Her questions tumble out, desperate for answers that might deny what she fears.

Chelsea responds with a sad smile. "Yes, we got married the next day. When I found out I was pregnant a few months later, I ... I wasn't sure if the baby – you — was Jon's or Travis's."

Krystal tries to speak, but the words catch in her throat. "Then how... why..." she begins, but again, she falls silent.

Chelsea reaches out, her eyes filled with affection. "We were so excited when we found out we were having a baby, Kris," she says softly. "When you were born, Jon was over the moon. He took a couple of months off work just to stay home and play with you. He adored you from the moment he held you."

Krystal's eyes fill with tears. She remains silent, her chest tight, waiting for her mother to continue.

"But …" Chelsea hesitates, her voice wavering. "During your six-month checkup, Jon read your blood report. It said you were type A."

Krystal's mind races, the pieces falling into place. As a biology major, she doesn't need her mother to explain further, but Chelsea continues, her voice barely above a whisper.

"Jon's blood type is O, and mine is B. O and B can't produce a child with type A blood. The only way for you to have type A is if one of your parents is type A … and that isn't Jon."

The silence between them is heavy, broken only by Krystal's sharp intake of breath as she processes the truth she had been so desperate to deny.

Chelsea's faint smile is tinged with sadness as she continues, her voice soft. "At that time, I had to tell him about me and Travis. Surprisingly, your dad was incredibly forgiving, Kris. When he learned the truth, he promised me he would treat you as his own. And he's kept that promise every single day. He truly loves you."

She pauses, her gaze softening with tenderness. "But I always knew, deep down, that he wanted a child of our own."

Krystal hesitates, then finally voices the question weighing on her heart. "Why didn't you?" Her voice is quiet, almost hesitant.

Chelsea lowers her eyes, her expression clouded with emotion. "We wanted to, Kris. Both of us did. But..." She pauses, struggling to find the right words. "After you were born, there were complications. The doctor warned me that trying for another child would put me at a very high risk of placental abruption. He said it wouldn't be safe for me, no matter how much I wanted it." Her voice trembles, the weight of unfulfilled dreams evident in her tone.

The words linger heavily in the silence, each one carrying a weight that presses on both of them. Chelsea forces a small smile, trying to soften the moment. "So, in the end, we poured all our love into you. Over time, I realized something: for Jon, you were enough."

Krystal's eyes fill with tears as she takes in her mother's words. The blend of love, regret, and sacrifice sinks deeply into her heart, leaving her both moved and overwhelmed. "Thank you, Mom," she whispers, her voice trembling with emotion but filled with gratitude.

~ ~ ~ ~ ~

Chapter 7
Encounter, Reveal, Suspicion

The next morning, Chelsea drives Krystal to school, just like she always does. As they pull into the parking lot, Brandon is already waiting nearby.

The moment Krystal steps out of the car, Brandon walks over, his eyes lighting up when he sees her. Without a word, he takes her hand, then turns to Chelsea with a respectful nod and a grateful smile. Chelsea returns the gesture, her expression warm and approving, before watching them head off together.

With a quiet smile of her own, Chelsea drives away, comforted by the sight of her daughter in good hands.

As Krystal walks beside Brandon toward the classroom, she glances at him, her voice hesitant. "Do you want to know what really happened between my parents?"

Brandon looks at her with a reassuring smile. "Only if you want to tell me," he says softly. "Every family has its own story, and some things are meant to stay private. You don't have to share unless you feel comfortable."

His thoughtful response soothes her unease, lifting a small weight off her shoulders. For a moment, she feels a sense of relief, knowing she doesn't have to carry it alone.

— ✦ —

Chelsea stops by a coffee shop, craving coffee and a cinnamon roll after a long night with Krystal. But as soon as she steps in, she spots Jon and Samantha deep in conversation at a corner table.

Her appetite vanishes instantly. She freezes, instinctively she wants to turn around.

"Why should I?" a voice inside her challenges. *"Why should I let them intimidate me?"*

Straightening herself, she walks over to their table and says calmly, "Good morning, Samantha. Good morning, Jon."

Upon seeing her, Samantha waves enthusiastically. "Hi Chelsea, good morning! Did you just drop Krystal off at school? Would you like to join us?" Her friendliness catches Chelsea off guard, leaving her momentarily stunned. She glances at Jon, who sits quietly with a faint smile.

Before Chelsea can respond, a stylish young woman emerges from the powder room. "Good morning, Mrs. Perkins," she says politely. Chelsea quickly recognizes her as Vanessa, the fashion design manager from Jon's department store.

Jon speaks up. "Samantha is looking for a custom dress for a special occasion, so I asked Vanessa to join us and see if our store could create something for her."

Then, turning to Chelsea, he asks, "Would you like to join us?"

Chelsea hesitates, unable to read his tone. After a brief moment, she shakes her head. "No, I'd better get going. Thanks for the offer."

As she leaves the coffee shop, an uneasy feeling settles over her, as though she's just lost a battle she didn't even realize she was fighting.

"The custom dress is the wedding dress," the thought strikes her instinctively, unfiltered. *"They're already talking about her wedding dress, as if I've agreed to the divorce. But what could I have said in that moment?"*

Her mind races as she walks away, the weight of the unspoken words pressing heavily on her chest.

Back at Einstein High, Krystal sits quietly next to Brandon on a bench during recess, her thoughts swirling. She hasn't told him her mom's story yet. Deep down, she fears he might see her differently if he knows she's the daughter of a disbanded rock duo, not the child of a wealthy banker. But another voice inside her urges her to share. *"Brandon cares so much about me. Should I really keep this from him?"* she wonders.

Brandon, sensing her inner turmoil, breaks the silence with a warm smile.

"My birthday's coming up," he says. "Let's have a beach party this weekend. I'll see if Katie and Charlie can join us too."

His cheerful suggestion pulls her out of her thoughts, and she looks at him, grateful for the distraction.

— ✦ —

Come Saturday morning. A lively group of youngsters gathers at the beach, dressed in their swimsuits and ready for a day of fun. Brandon, organizing the outing, brings along his younger sister, Caitlin, who insisted on inviting her best friend, Tiffany, to join them.

Brandon's younger brother, Brett, opted to stay home, being more of an introvert and still recovering from a recent stomach infection.

When Tiffany's mom drops her off, she can't help but notice Krystal standing nearby. *"I thought Brit was stunning, but this girl is just as beautiful,"* she muses, mentally comparing Krystal to her younger sister. *"But why does she have such a sad look in her eyes?"*

Her curiosity lingers as she drives away, leaving the group to spread out along the sandy shore. Their laughter and chatter blend with the sound of the waves, filling the air with the carefree joy of a perfect beach day.

Tiffany approaches Charlie and Katie with a bright smile. "Hi, Katie! Hi, Charlie! It's been ages! How have you guys been?" she greets enthusiastically.

Katie beams at her. "Oh, Tiffany! The last time we saw you, you were just five. Look at you now—so tall and pretty, just like Auntie Kelsi!"

Charlie lingers quietly behind Katie's wheelchair, but she notices and waves him off with a warm laugh. "You don't have to stick with me, Charlie. Go join them and have fun," she says playfully. "Show them you're the best swimmer out there!"

Tiffany takes the cue, pulling Charlie along to introduce him to Caitlin. Meanwhile, Katie wheels herself to a shady spot under a tree, turning her chair away from the group. She removes her goggles, closes her eyes, and tilts her face upward, soaking in the sunlight to catch some tan.

74

While Brandon chats with Charlie, Tiffany, and Caitlin near the water, Krystal notices Katie reclining peacefully in her wheelchair under the shade of a tree. Intrigued, she walks over, grabs a beach chair, and sits down beside her.

Katie, eyes closed and a soft smile on her lips, radiates an effortless calm. As Krystal watches her, she feels a mix of admiration and curiosity. *"She's no prettier than me, but why... why is she so captivating?"* The question lingers in her mind, unanswered.

Katie opens her eyes, catching Krystal's gaze. "Hi, Krystal. Want to join me? I'm not exactly the active type, so I like to find some peace and quiet wherever I go," she says with a warm smile.

"Me too," Krystal replies with a soft sigh, her eyes drifting toward Brandon and Charlie in the distance. "I really appreciate Brandon organizing this outing. He's done so much for me, especially with everything I'm going through right now."

Katie tilts her head thoughtfully. "That night, when you told me you were staying home with your mom... did you manage to sort out your worries?" she asks gently. "You look more relaxed now, Krystal. Hopefully, things are getting better."

Krystal pauses for a moment, reflecting on Katie's words, and gives a small nod, her heart feeling lighter in Katie's calm presence.

As they chat, two young men start walking toward them, clearly drawn by the sight of the two beautiful girls. Krystal notices their approach and immediately feels a sense of unease, silently raising her guard. Katie, on the other hand, remains calm, her composure unshaken.

"Hey, sweetie pie, what a shame to sit here all alone. Let us keep you company," one of the guys teases, his eyes fixed on Krystal, "I'm Marco, what's yours?" He laughs as he steps closer, while his friend stares at Katie.

Krystal reacts instantly, standing up and stepping back. "We have company," she says firmly, raising her voice slightly. "Hey, Brandon! Come here."

Meanwhile, Katie stays seated in her wheelchair, her expression as serene as ever. She knows she has taken off her goggles. She meets the second guy's gaze with the same calm, inviting smile she had shown to Brock, a quiet confidence radiating from her. It's clear she isn't intimidated, her demeanor as composed as if she were alone on the beach.

Marco glances back and notices two guys and two girls approaching. Sensing trouble, he grabs his friend's arm, but he seems frozen, mesmerized by Katie's calm, serene gaze. Frustrated, Marco steps between them, blocking the stare, and signals to his friend with a sharp look — it's time to go.

Brandon quickly steps protectively in front of Krystal, his eyes locked on Marco. "What's going on?" he asks firmly.

Marco glances around, sizing up the group. He notes that there are only two men, and one of them is wearing goggles, suggesting possible vision issues. *"Chip and I can handle this,"* he thinks. He smirks at Krystal. "She's too pretty for you. Let's play winner-takes-all," he says, taking a boxer's stance.

Brandon shakes his head, calm but resolute. "I'm not playing your game. Please just leave." He grabs Krystal's hand and signals Charlie to wheel Katie away.

Marco blocks their path, his tone escalating. "Come on, punk!" he shouts, throwing a punch.

What he doesn't realize is that Brandon has years of MMA training and has won junior tournaments before. Within seconds, he is thrown into the sand twice, his confidence quickly evaporating.

Furious, he scrambles to his feet again. As Brandon shakes his head and turns to walk away, Marco lunges, throwing a handful of sand into Brandon's face.

Momentarily blinded, Brandon raises one hand to protect his eyes and the other defensively to his chest, but he's caught off guard by a heavy blow to his abdomen, followed by a solid punch to his face. Brandon stumbles backward and falls to the ground.

Marco steps forward, raising his foot to stomp on Brandon. But before it lands, it's blocked mid-air by another foot – of a young man with a pair of goggles on his face. The impact sends him stumbling backward, momentarily off balance.

Anger overtakes him completely, and in a flash, he pulls out a switchblade.

"Watch out, Charlie!" All the girls scream, as Marco is lunging at Charlie. Charlie reacts quickly, flicking his arm up and grabbing the attacker's wrist, but not before the blade slices through his arm, leaving a six-inch wound. Blood trickles down, but Charlie doesn't flinch.

As the girls' screams echo, Charlie twists Marco's arm with practiced precision, forcing him to drop the knife into the sand.

At that moment, his friend Chip snaps out of his trance from staring at Katie and, seeing his companion in trouble, charges at Charlie with fury. But Charlie meets him head-on with a swift, sharp kick. Barefoot on the beach, Charlie's toes land like a blunt axe against Chip's chest, sending him flying backward several feet as he crashes face-first into the sand.

Marco struggles against Charlie's iron grip, but Charlie calmly flicks his wrist and releases him. Before the girls can cheer in relief, Charlie turns his attention to Brandon, walking over to help him up.

Marco picks up the fallen switchblade and glares at Charlie's back, his anger simmering.

"Don't even think about it," Katie's voice cuts through the tension, calm but commanding. "Don't do something you'll regret, Marco," she says, calling him out by name.

Marco turns toward Katie and meets her unwavering gaze. A wave of shame washes over him. Without another word, he walks over to help Chip to his feet. Together, they trudge away in silence, leaving the group behind.

Tiffany and Caitlin rush over to Charlie, quickly tending to his wound. They bandage it with care, their actions filled with both appreciation and admiration for his bravery. Meanwhile, Krystal kneels beside Brandon, gently using a wet towel to wipe the sand from his eyes. Though her heart is fully with Brandon, she finds herself stealing a few glances at Charlie.

Katie sits quietly in her wheelchair, observing the scene with a small smile. She's happy for Krystal, knowing she has someone like Brandon who cares deeply and stands up for her. *"Regardless of what happens with her parents, she'll be fine,"* Katie thinks, reassured.

Yet, a twinge of envy creeps in. *"I have Charlie watching out for me, but he's my brother,"* she reflects, her gaze drifting to Tiffany and Caitlin fussing over him. *"In a few years, he'll have Amanda — or maybe someone else — to care for. Then it won't be me he's looking out for anymore."*

She lets out a quiet sigh, the thought weighing on her as she watches the others.

Just then, Krystal's phone rings. She picks it up, saying, "Hi Mom…" while waving toward Katie and pointing to Brandon as she steps back to take the call.

Katie wheels herself over to Brandon, helping him sit up. She picks up the towel Krystal left behind and gently continues cleaning the sand from his face.

Brandon slowly opens his eyes. The first thing he sees is a serene, caring and beautiful face before him. It's not Krystal — and the girl is sitting in a wheelchair.

"Katie? Is that you? I almost didn't recognize you without your goggles," Brandon says, his tone filled with genuine surprise.

Katie smiles warmly. "Oh, I just took them off to get some sun," she replies. Then, with a grateful look, she adds, "Thanks for standing up for us, Brandon."

Brandon nods and glances over at Charlie, who is now surrounded by Tiffany and Caitlin, both animatedly chatting. Marco and Chip were gone, and Charlie quietly smiles at the two girls, seemingly at ease.

"Actually, I have to thank Charlie for saving me," Brandon admits, a hint of unease in his voice. "He's... how can he defend himself so well? That was incredible!"

Katie smiles proudly. "He's been training since he was six," she explains. "He used to get bullied by his classmates, so our uncle, who's a Taekwondo black belt, started training him. And Charlie's been dedicated to it ever since."

"He must be working very hard." Brandon nods. Although he hadn't witnessed the confrontation himself, the tension of what had transpired lingers in his mind. Even without words, Charlie's actions had spoken volumes. A strange, faint bitterness stirs within him as he tries to make sense of the emotions rising in him.

Krystal returns to the group, phone in hand. Her eyes immediately land on Katie and Brandon, sitting close and smiling warmly at each other. Katie is without her goggles, and there's a radiance to her that Krystal can't ignore.

A sudden, unspoken wave of jealousy tugs at her heart without any warning. She forces a smile, but the feeling lingers, unsettling and unfamiliar.

Brandon notices her return and looks at her. "Your mom called?" he asks casually, hoping she'll open up and share something with him and Katie. After all, they're her closest friends.

Krystal hesitates, glancing briefly at Katie before answering. "Nothing much. She just said she'll be late coming home and asked me to prepare dinner if I get back early." Her voice is calm, but inside, she feels an inexplicable hesitation — a reluctance to fully open up in front of the two of them.

As the day winds down, everyone is worn out from the activities. Tiffany is picked up by her mother, while Katie and Charlie board a bus to head home.

Krystal and Caitlin climb into Brandon's car. "Caitlin, I'll drop you off first, then I'll take Krystal home," Brandon says, hoping to have some private time with Krystal afterward.

But Krystal surprises him. "That won't be necessary, Brandon. You can drop me off first and then go home to rest. It's been a long day."

Her response catches Brandon completely off guard. He senses something is off but chooses to respect her decision. When they arrive at Krystal's house, he parks, steps out to open the door for her, and watches as she gets out.

Carrying her backpack, Krystal walks toward the entrance without saying a word, leaving Brandon standing by his car, deeply puzzled.

~ ~ ~ ~ ~

Chapter 8
Torn

Once Krystal steps into the empty mansion, she rushes to her bedroom, throws down her backpack, and collapses onto her bed. Covering her face with a pillow, she begins to weep, her quiet sobs soon turning into uncontrollable crying. Tears soak into the pillow.

Chelsea had told her earlier that she would be away for a few days, trusting Brandon to take care of her daughter. She'd also suggested Krystal spend time with Katie to share her feelings, just as she did last week. She needed some time to herself, she said, to work through her own stress.

Before today, Krystal would have embraced the idea wholeheartedly. Spending quality time with two trusted friends felt like exactly what she needed.

But everything changed during the phone call earlier. She had glanced up just in time to see Brandon open his eyes — and the stunned look on his face as he stared at Katie. It was a look Krystal recognized all too well, the same one she'd seen from countless guys before: that mix of awe and captivation. It reminded her of the way Chip had stared at Katie, except Brandon showed far more restraint.

The memory resurfaced again — the moment Katie had stopped Marco from stabbing Charlie. Her poise and unwavering confidence in that critical instant had been magnetic, almost impossible to look away from. She couldn't deny it: Katie's presence was undeniably commanding, the kind that effortlessly drew admiration from everyone around her, especially men.

And now, Krystal found herself questioning everything. She recalls the way Brandon and Katie looked at each other, the easy flow of their conversation, the subtle energy between them just before she had returned. It wasn't overt, but it was enough to stir something deep within her — a gnawing uncertainty she couldn't ignore.

She had trusted Brandon completely ever since they started dating, but now, for the first time, doubt creeps into her heart. She isn't sure if she could trust her own feelings anymore.

"My parents are going through a divorce, and now my best friend is stealing my boyfriend!" The thought overwhelms her, each word echoing like a fresh wound.

She feels the weight of it pressing down on her chest, a suffocating burden she couldn't escape.

She just couldn't cope.

— ✦ —

On the way back home, Caitlin chats animatedly while Brandon focuses on the road.

"Charlie is amazing! He fought off two big guys like it was nothing," she exclaims, her voice brimming with excitement. "And guess what? He's actually blind! He has to rely on those goggles to tell him what to do. Can you believe that?"

"I know," Brandon replies quietly, his tone subdued. He can't quite explain it, but every time Charlie comes up in conversation, it leaves him with a faint sense of unease.

Today has been no different. The fact that he's been saved by someone so young — and with a severe visual impairment – is hard to reconcile. It isn't jealousy or resentment exactly, but it stirs something in him he doesn't entirely understand: an uncomfortable awareness of his own vulnerability.

That night, as he lies in bed, his mind races.

He's always been the confident one, secure in his role as an athlete, a provider, and a protector for Krystal. But not tonight. Tonight, the defeat doesn't come from Marco — it comes from Charlie. *How did that even happen?*

His thoughts shift to Krystal. *What happened to her?* He wonders aloud. It's the first time she's acted like this — distant and withdrawn. She barely spoke to me and avoided spending any private time together after we left the beach. *Why is she mad at me? Did I do something wrong? Is it because I cannot protect her?* He asks himself, frustration mingling with confusion.

And then, suddenly, an image flashes in his mind: Katie, smiling without her goggles, sitting in her wheelchair. There's a warmth in her smile, a serene confidence that seems to radiate peace, reaching a part of him he hasn't realized is yearning for something deeper.

She isn't prettier than Krystal — not by conventional standards — but there is something about her calm and steady demeanor, a quiet strength that Krystal lacks. It isn't just her smile; it is the way she carries herself, unshaken and self-assured, that stirs something unfamiliar and unsettling within him.

Brandon shakes his head, trying to dismiss the thought. *Why am I even thinking about this? It's not right...*

Closing his eyes, he takes a deep breath and begins to pray, searching for clarity amidst the confusion swirling in his heart.

— ✦ —

Back at Katie's home, she carefully examines Charlie's arm.

"Oh, the cut isn't too deep. You'll be fine," she says playfully. A teasing smile spreads across her face. "Look at you, though — two beautiful girls taking care of you. Totally worth it! If Amanda were here, she'd be so jealous."

Charlie laughs shyly. "I wish Amanda were with us too, but this isn't really our party." Then, lowering his voice, he adds, "Brandon was a little careless. That guy's no match for him. He just played tricks using sand."

Katie nods, her expression softening. "Yeah, Brandon could've won easily. It's unfair." She sighs, her tone tinged with disappointment.

"Hey, Sis," Charlie says after a moment, his voice more serious. "I noticed Krystal was unusually quiet after talking to her mom. I hope she's okay."

Katie pauses, her teasing smile fading as concern creeps into her eyes. "Yeah... I noticed that too. Something's definitely bothering her."

As the realization sinks in, Katie recalls Krystal's earlier explanation about her mom's call. It hadn't been convincing. There had to be something else — something Krystal wasn't sharing. Being her closest friend, she feels it's her duty to reach out, to offer a listening ear and help lighten whatever burden Krystal is carrying.

Katie picks up her phone and calls Krystal. The phone rings endlessly, but no one answers.

A sense of unease washes over her. At a time like this, she would expect Brandon to be by Krystal's side, ready to pick up her phone if she didn't, just like he had done before. But this time, there's only silence.

Katie frowns, her concern growing. She waits ten minutes and tries calling again, but the result is the same — no answer.

Her worry deepens. Feeling a need to act, she scrolls through her call log and finds Brandon's number from the time he called to invite her to the beach. Without hesitation, she dials him.

As the phone rings, her fingers tap anxiously on the armrest of her wheelchair. *Please pick up*, she silently pleads.

Brandon is trying to take his mind off Katie when the phone rings. He glances at the screen and answers quickly.

"Hey, Brandon," Katie's voice comes through, tinged with urgency. "I've been trying to reach Krystal, but

89

she's not answering my calls. Did you drop her off at home?"

Brandon sits up straight. "Yeah, I dropped her off a while ago," he says, his tone matching her urgency. "I saw her walk into her house. But… something seemed off. She wasn't talking to me, not even saying good night. That's not like her."

Katie falls silent on the other end, her unspoken worry mirroring his.

"She's usually not like this, Katie," Brandon continues after a short pause. "Something's really bothering her. I'm going to drop by and check on her." He hesitates briefly before adding, "You want to come along too? I'll pick you up first."

He's not entirely sure why he wants Katie to come, but in the moment, it feels like the right thing to do.

Katie hesitates, uncertainty flickering in her mind. "Yes, pick me up then," she says softly, her voice betraying her own doubts.

Neither of them knows how Krystal will react to seeing them together. The last thing she might want is for the two people causing her turmoil to show up side by side. Yet, caught up in their shared concern, they fail to realize that they themselves are the source of her distress.

— ✦ —

Chelsea sits alone in the upscale hotel bar, a half-empty glass of wine in front of her, lost in thought. Her mind circles around Jon, Samantha, and Travis, each name stirring a different mix of emotions.

The bar, nestled in an affluent area, isn't a typical singles' spot. Yet, Chelsea is a very attractive woman, a more matured version of Krystal. A few men have tried their luck, but her experience in the entertainment world has made it easy to fend them off with grace.

As she considers a final drink before calling it a night, her phone buzzes. Glancing at the screen, she's surprised to see Brandon's name. She answers, "Brandon?"

"Yes, Auntie, it's me," Brandon says, his voice strained. "We found Krystal unconscious—she swallowed a whole bottle of sleeping pills. We're in the ER right now."

Chelsea freezes, her heart pounding. "She tried to kill herself? What happened? I thought you were all at a beach party today! How did it come to this?"

Her questions come in a rapid-fire rush, each one a desperate plea for answers Brandon doesn't have.

"Auntie, where are you?" Brandon's voice is urgent, almost pleading. "Please come over as soon as possible. We're at U.C. Medical."

"I'm a few hours away," Chelsea replies as she glances at the empty glass on the bar. She knows she can't drive after her drinks. "I'll come by first thing in the morning. In the meantime, keep a close eye on her." After a pause, she adds firmly, "Call me immediately if anything changes."

As she hangs up, a new thought strikes her — she should call Jon. *Jon is her father, and he loves her so much. But… he's divorcing me because he wants another child. Would he even care anymore?*

She knows she ought to call him, yet a nagging voice inside her whispers to keep Krystal away from Jon. The bitterness of their separation lingers, clouding her judgment.

Her hand trembles slightly as she picks up the phone, her finger hovering over the screen. But she hesitates, uncertainty and conflict holding her back.

Back in the Emergency Room lobby, Katie sits beside Brandon on the bench. Brandon's car couldn't accommodate a wheelchair, so she just grabbed her crutches and come along.

As Brandon hangs up the phone, Katie speaks calmly. "Auntie can't come right now, can she? That's understandable. She's dealing with so much." After a pause, she adds with quiet resolve, "I'll stay as long as I have to. You should go home and rest, Brandon. There are things girls may not want to share when boys are around."

Brandon is struck by Katie's insight and empathy. Her understanding of the situation impresses him, but he can't bring himself to leave her alone in the waiting room.

"When Krystal wakes up, you can go in and check on her," he says gently. "I'll stay out here in the lobby."

Here they sit, quietly looking at each other.

Just then, a nurse steps into the lobby and says, "The patient just woke up. She's a little confused. You can go in and talk to her."

Katie grips her crutches and rises to her feet. "I'll go in. You stay here, Brandon," she says softly before making her way toward the patient area, her movements deliberate but steady.

As Brandon watches Katie's figure disappear down the hallway, his mind begins to race, thoughts swirling in a storm of concern, guilt, and something he can't quite name.

He recalls the moment he arrived at Katie's house and realized his car couldn't accommodate a wheelchair. He hesitated briefly, but before he could offer an alternative,

Katie had already wheeled herself to grab her crutches. *"Let's go,"* she said, quick and determined, leaving no room for doubt.

Then, his thoughts shift to Krystal. He remembers the intimate moment they shared when she gave him the code to her house. *"Whenever you want to sneak in to see me, you can,"* she had said, her voice playful but trusting. She had entrusted him with access to her sanctuary — her home.

The memory of finding Krystal unconscious in her bedroom resurfaces. Before he could even think to call 9-1-1, Katie had already hobbled over, checking Krystal's eyes, breathing, pulse and heartbeat with calm precision. She then quickly scanned the nightstand and spotted the empty bottle of pills. Turning to him, she spoke in a steady voice to calm him down: *"She's overdosed, but her vitals are stable. Let's wait for the paramedics."* Her decisive actions left him profoundly impressed.

As they waited for the paramedics, his gaze lingered on Krystal. The sadness etched on her face and the dried tears on her cheeks struck him deeply, stirring emotions he couldn't ignore.

It is undeniable: these two girls each holds a place in his heart — perhaps in different ways, perhaps in separate corners — but both were deeply rooted there, immovable and significant.

~ ~ ~ ~ ~

Chapter 9
Two Hearts, Three Souls

As Katie makes her way toward Krystal's patient room, her mind races too.

She recalls the moment the paramedics arrived. Without hesitation, she opted to stay with Krystal in the ambulance while Brandon followed in his car. She didn't want Krystal to wake up alone, and she wanted to be there for her, just in case.

Sitting beside Krystal in the ambulance, she remembers taking out a bracelet she had picked up from Krystal's bedroom while Brandon was busy explaining the situation to the paramedics. It was an inexpensive, fake jade bracelet made of plastic — something Katie had bought during a trip to Mexico. She had given it to Krystal as a birthday present, knowing she couldn't afford anything more elegant.

Yet, despite its simplicity, she noticed that Krystal always wore it whenever they met. Even that day at the beach, it had been on her wrist. Katie knew the bracelet wasn't valuable or stylish, but it carried a deeper significance—it was a silent testament to their unspoken friendship, a bond that she now realized Krystal cherished.

But tonight, when Katie found the bracelet on the floor of Krystal's bedroom, it was deeply scratched, trampled, and missing a small piece.

A wave of unease washed over her. *"She took it off and tried to break it!"* The thought frightened her. *"This bracelet is a token of our friendship, and now she wants to throw it away. She's so angry at me!"*

Her eyes grew wet as she struggled to understand why, the weight of her fear and guilt pressing heavily on her heart.

She reaches Krystal's room and hesitates at the door, unsure if she should go in. Finally, she takes a deep breath, bites her lip, and gently pushes the door open.

Meanwhile, Brandon sits in the lobby, finishing his third cup of coffee. He glances at the clock. *Why hasn't she come out yet?* He wonders, his fingers tapping nervously on the armrest of his chair.

Just then, he notices Katie walking slowly into the lobby, leaning on her crutches. Brandon stands up immediately, his concern evident. "Did you see her? How does she look? Why would she do this to herself?"

His words tumble out, his voice filled with urgency and desperation.

Katie approaches the bench and sits down, her expression heavy with concern.

"When I walked in, a doctor was attending her," she begins softly, her voice tinged with emotion. She pauses briefly, gathering her thoughts. "The doctor asked her some general questions, but she wasn't responding at all. Her stare was hollow, like she couldn't recognize anything — where she is, why she's here... even me." Katie's voice falters, and she wipes at the tears welling in her eyes.

After a moment, she continues, her tone quieter. "The doctor stepped outside with me and explained. Krystal has dissociative amnesia — a temporary memory loss caused by a traumatic event. They recommend she stay in the hospital under observation for a few days. Hopefully, her mom will come by then."

Katie exhales deeply, her words lingering in the air as she looks down, trying to compose herself.

Hearing her account, Brandon feels his chest tighten. *A traumatic event that triggers amnesia?* The phrase loops in his mind, stirring an instinctive sense of guilt. Could it be about him? He doesn't know, but the uncertainty gnaws at him.

"All we can do now is wait, Katie," he says, his voice measured but uneasy. After a pause, he adds, "Maybe I should take you home so you can rest."

But Katie shakes her head gently, her eyes closing as she responds, "I can't leave her here alone. Not until I see her mom." Her tone is soft but resolute. "You should go home, Brandon."

Brandon studies her for a moment, her exhaustion evident despite her composure. He can't bring himself to leave her like this. "I'll stay with you," he says firmly, taking a seat beside her. Something about being near her feels right — comforting, even amidst the worry.

After a long and emotionally draining day, Katie finally begins to succumb to her exhaustion. Her head dips slightly, and she dozes off, unconsciously leaning toward Brandon. Without hesitation, he shifts closer, turning to let her head rest on his broad shoulder.

For a moment, the waiting room is still, save for the quiet rhythm of their breathing, as Brandon sits silently, offering her a sense of steady, unspoken support.

As dawn breaks, Chelsea's car pulls into the hospital parking lot. After a quick consultation with the nurses at the registration desk, she makes her way quickly toward the patient area lobby.

The first sight that greets her stops her in her tracks —
a young woman's head resting gently on Brandon's
shoulder as they sit on a bench, both with their eyes
closed. Brandon's left hand is clasped around the girl's
right hand in an unmistakably tender gesture.

Chelsea's eyes narrow slightly as she studies the girl.
She's strikingly pretty, her features calm and serene
even in rest. Chelsea racks her brain. She's seen Katie a
few times before, but always with those thick, heavy
goggles that seemed to define her appearance. Now,
without them, she fails to recognize that the girl beside
Brandon is Katie.

Her chest tightens with a mix of confusion and unease.
"Who is this girl?" she wonders silently. The scene stirs a
pang of discomfort — she had seen Brandon holding
Krystal's hand and resting together like this before, but
this time it's not Krystal's hand he's holding.

Katie suddenly stirs awake, her eyes fluttering open.
Realizing Chelsea is approaching, she quickly lifts her
head up and withdraws her hand from Brandon's, her
cheeks flushing slightly. Almost simultaneously,
Brandon wakes up, straightening himself in his seat as
he notices Chelsea.

"Good morning, Auntie Chelsea," Brandon greets, his
voice tinged with embarrassment.

"How's Krystal? You stayed here overnight?" Chelsea questions Brandon, her gaze shifting attentively to Katie.

Katie grips her crutches and stands up immediately, offering a polite but slightly embarrassed smile. "She's okay, Auntie Chelsea. We were waiting for you to come and see her," she responds softly.

Chelsea recognizes Katie's voice instantly. She's surprised. "Katie? You can walk now?" She's momentarily taken aback, not only by seeing Katie without her wheelchair but also by how stunning she looks without her goggles. The transformation is striking, and for a moment, Chelsea struggles to reconcile this image with the Katie she remembers.

Out of politeness, she refrains from commenting further on Katie's appearance, keeping her expression neutral. But deep inside, an uncomfortable feeling surfaces, an inexplicable unease that she can't quite put into words.

The three of them walk into Krystal's room. On the cart next to her bed sits a tray with milk, toast, and a banana. Krystal is lying on the bed, her face turned away from the door.

"Hi, sweetie, it's me," Chelsea says softly as she approaches the bed and gently pats Krystal on the shoulder.

Krystal turns to see her mom, and without a word, she buries her face into Chelsea's arms, her tears flowing freely.

Chelsea strokes her daughter's hair and whispers soothingly. Then, she lifts her head slightly and says, "Look who else is here to see you."

Krystal turns her head slowly, her eyes settling on Brandon and Katie. Her silent gaze carries an unspoken depth, stirring an ache in Chelsea's heart. It's a look Chelsea recognizes instantly—a haunting echo of Jon's expression two years ago when he had noticed her staring at Travis on the stage.

In that moment, Chelsea understands everything. She knows her daughter too well to miss the unspoken pain in her eyes. Leaning toward Brandon, she whispers softly but firmly, "You two should head home and get some rest. I'll take care of her from here."

Katie and Brandon walk out in silence, each lost in their thoughts.

Katie replays the moment just before she drifted off to sleep. She had felt a warm hand tenderly clasping hers. Though her mind told her to pull away, her heart refused. For the first time, she allowed herself to enjoy the warmth and closeness, a sensation she had never experienced before.

Brandon, too, is mesmerized by the same moment. He remembers being wide awake after too much coffee, fully aware of Katie's head resting gently on his shoulder. They had never felt so close before. Perhaps it was their shared concern and care for Krystal that brought them together. But deep down, he wondered if it was something more.

Looking at Katie's face so closely had stirred something unfamiliar within him, something he couldn't explain. For a fleeting moment, he realized — he wanted to kiss her.

But suddenly, it felt as though Katie's voice echoed in his mind: *"Don't even think about it! Don't do something you'll regret!"* The same words she had firmly said to Marco now resonated in his thoughts, halting him.

He exhaled deeply, a quiet sigh of restraint mingled with the ache of unspoken emotions. Even so, an irresistible pull lingered within him. He slowly reached out for her hand, as though drawn by the warmth and connection they had shared earlier.

As Brandon drives Katie home, the silence between them is thick with unspoken thoughts. Concern for Krystal's well-being weighs heavily, but so do the emotions stirred during their time in the hospital lobby. Both replay Krystal's gaze, heavy with unspoken feelings, and Chelsea's quiet yet deliberate suggestion for them to leave. The shared memory hangs in the air, unacknowledged but undeniable.

When they arrive at Katie's home, Brandon pauses for a moment before getting out. Their eyes meet briefly, but neither speaks. In that shared glance, an understanding passes between them — they both know why Krystal is so deeply upset, why her behavior has been so withdrawn. The weight of the realization presses down on them, unspoken yet painfully clear.

Katie finally breaks the silence. "When we were in Krystal's bedroom, I saw the bracelet I gave her," she begins quietly, her voice trembling slightly as she looks away. "She'd taken it off… and tried to break it." Her gaze drops further. "She's really mad at me." She pauses, hoping Brandon might respond, but he remains quiet, his thoughts unreadable.

She grabs her crutches as she tries to opens the car door to get out. Brandon immediately gets off from his seat, walks over and open her door, extending his hand to her. For a fleeting moment, her hand touches his. But then, as if startled by her own action, she pulls back and grips her crutches instead.

The small gesture speaks louder than words. In that subtle moment, the emotions both are trying to suppress rise to the surface—unspoken, unresolved, yet undeniably present.

Katie grips her crutches tightly, hobbling slowly toward her front door. Brandon lingers a few steps behind, torn by hesitation. He's accustomed to embracing Krystal when dropping her off, but tonight, it's not Krystal — yet the urge feels just as natural.

Katie reaches the door and pauses, turning back to face him. Her voice, calm but resolute, breaks the silence. "We should take some time to cool off, Brandon," she says softly but firmly. "I probably won't see Krystal for a while. Please... take care of her."

Before Brandon can respond, Katie steps inside quickly, closing the door behind her. Her back pressed against the door, tears spill silently down her cheeks — tears she doesn't want Brandon to see. Outside, Brandon stands motionless, the weight of her words and the emotion in her voice leaving him rooted to the spot.

Charlie steps out of his room as the sound of the door closing echoes through the hallway. He stops in his tracks when he sees Katie, her face streaked with tears, her shoulders shaking as she tries to suppress her sobs.

"Sis?" he calls softly, stepping closer. "What's wrong? Are you okay?"

He knows Brandon had taken her to see Krystal, and now, after an entire night, she's home in tears. Trusting that Brandon wouldn't have hurt her, he realizes something much deeper must have caused her pain.

Katie forces a faint smile, but the effort only emphasizes her sadness. She knows she can't hide her feelings from her brother.

"I just need some space, Charlie," she says quietly, her voice trembling. "We'll talk later, I promise."

Charlie hesitates, his concern evident, but he respects her need for solitude. Nodding gently, he retreats to his room, casting one last worried glance at his sister.

Katie hobbles into her room and collapses onto her bed. She's not the type to cry easily, but now her tears fall like rain, unchecked and unstoppable.

She realizes she's been admiring Brandon all along — his looks, his talents, and most of all, the genuine care he shows for everyone, not just Krystal.

Memories flood her mind: how he gently pulled Jake aside during the shootout tournament to let her pass, how he was the first to steady her wheelchair when Jake tried to topple it. Back then, she was just an unassuming girl, wearing thick goggles, sitting in a wheelchair.

And then there were the tender moments: the way she had revealed herself, gently touching his face and wiping the sand from his eyes on the beach; the look in his eyes when he opened them, filled with warmth and admiration; and the tender way he clasped her hand in the hospital lobby.

A girl's intuition whispers to her — he likes her, perhaps more than he should.

But he's her best friend's boyfriend.

She has always been jealous of Krystal, believing the only way to feel equal is to beat her in the debate. But now, there's more — she realizes she might have a chance to take her boyfriend.

The thought flashes through her mind, and it terrifies her.

~ ~ ~ ~ ~

Chapter 10
Light at Tunnel's End

Chelsea sits silently next to Krystal, watching as her daughter cries herself to sleep. Krystal hasn't spoken a word since the moment Chelsea, Brandon, and Katie entered the room, but as her mother, Chelsea feels the pain radiating from her — pain that's all too familiar.

She remembers the same anguish when Travis told her he was going to marry Melissa and that their paths must part. That haunting ache now resurfaces, this time through her daughter's heartbreak.

"How could this happen to my daughter?" she wonders, her gaze fixed on Krystal's tear-streaked, beautiful face. Her thoughts drift to Katie — not more beautiful, perhaps, but with a serene, confident charm that she knows Krystal lacks. The comparison lingers, unspoken but undeniable.

Chelsea sits quietly, humming as she strokes Krystal's hair, the familiar tune spilling from her lips:

"When all the others turn their backs and walk away
You can count on me to stay..."

Her voice wavers slightly but carries a tender strength, as if weaving a cocoon of comfort around her daughter. She had sung this song many times on stage after her band had broken up. Each time, she was thinking about Travis then. But this time, only her daughter is on her mind.

The song fills the quiet room, her voice reaching into the stillness.

"... And for all the times we've cried...
I always felt that God was on our side..."

A second voice gently joins hers, low and filled with raw emotion. The voice, though less refined than hers, resonates through the air. The raw intensity in his tone is undeniable, capable of moving even the most unyielding heart to tears.

Chelsea looks up as Jon steps into the room, his eyes locked on hers while her hand is still on Krystal's head.

Chelsea's mind swirls. She called him last night but he hadn't answered. All she could do was leave a voicemail, never expecting him to show up. Yet here he is, singing her song back to her.

"You and me against the world," she thinks, tears welling in her eyes. In that instant, the song becomes more than

just words; it transforms into a bridge — mending the distance between them and binding the scattered pieces of their love together.

"Is she alright, Chelsea?" Jon says softly as he slowly approaches Krystal's bed.

Before Chelsea can answer, Krystal stirs and murmurs, her voice faint. "Is that you, Dad?" Her eyes remain closed, and tears trace her cheeks as she continues, "I miss you, Dad…"

Jon moves closer, his hand gently resting on Krystal's hair. In a hushed tone, he whispers, "I miss you too. It won't be just you two against the world anymore," his hand brushing against Chelsea's.

Krystal grows still, her breathing steadying. Though she remains asleep, the sound of her father's voice weaves its way into her dreams, bringing a soft smile to her lips.

Krystal's peaceful smile fills both Chelsea and Jon with a sense of relief. Meeting Chelsea's eyes, Jon gives a slight nod and motions toward the door, silently asking her to step outside for a moment to talk.

Katie is still lying in bed when Charlie knocks gently on the door. "Sis, did something happen to Krystal? Do you want to talk about it?" he asks, his voice laced with concern.

Katie sits up, hastily wiping the tears from her face. "Come in, please," she says softly.

Charlie steps inside and sits on the edge of her bed. "Is Krystal okay? She seemed upset with Brandon. But why? He's always so nice to her." At just fourteen, Charlie remains unaware of the intricate emotional dynamics between boys and girls.

"She's not mad at Brandon, Charlie," Katie says after a moment of hesitation. "She's mad at me. She thinks I'm... stealing Brandon from her." Her voice cracks, and tears begin to stream down her cheeks once again.

"How could she? You're her best friend!" Charlie exclaims, disbelief written all over his face. Katie doesn't answer, her head hanging low, her silence speaking volumes—a quiet admission laced with guilt.

After a long pause, Katie finally musters the courage to speak. "Krystal tried to kill herself," she says, her voice trembling. "She swallowed sleeping pills. We rushed her to the hospital and stayed there until her mom arrived." She takes a deep breath, struggling to steady herself before continuing. "The doctor said she's suffering from temporary memory loss."

Charlie is left speechless. Katie hadn't defended herself against Krystal's accusation, and that silence weighed heavily in the air. To him, his sister is nothing short of a faultless angel — kind, selfless, and incapable of wrongdoing. How could someone like her hurt her best friend? The thought felt impossible, yet here it was, pressing down on him like an unbearable weight.

It seems Katie can read her brother's thoughts. Taking a deep breath, she speaks softly, "Yes, I like Brandon, and I think he likes me too."

She pauses, trying to steady herself, and continues with a trace of composure. "But I'm not stealing Brandon from her, Charlie. I would never do that. All I know is that Brandon cares about Krystal so much that no one could ever take him away from her. And honestly, I don't even know how she figured out that we like each other."

Her voice quivers, caught between guilt and frustration, as she looks down, unable to meet her brother's wide, questioning gaze.

Charlie sits still, struggling to find the right words to comfort his sister. He hates seeing her so weighed down by guilt and sadness, and he can't just sit there doing nothing.

Suddenly, a memory surfaces — Tiffany's words at the beach. *"Mom and Dad will be so happy to see you. You are the living testimony of Dad's greatest invention of all time!"*

A spark of hope lights up in his mind. "Hey, Sis," he says earnestly, breaking the silence. "Why don't we pay Uncle Fraser and Auntie Kelsi a visit? Uncle Fraser is the wisest man we've ever known. He might have some advice that could help you."

Katie opens her eyes, her gaze softening as she considers his suggestion. After a moment, she nods slightly. "That's a good idea," she murmurs. "We haven't seen them in a while. And if it weren't for Uncle Fraser, who knows where we'd be now."

A faint smile appears on her face, a glimmer of relief in her expression, as she starts to feel the weight lifting ever so slightly.

Brandon lies in his bed, staring at the ceiling, unable to find rest after the emotionally charged night at the hospital. His mind refuses to settle, replaying the haunting images from the evening.

Krystal's despairing expression when she saw him with Katie in her hospital room lingers vividly, a painful reminder of her fragile state. Then there's Katie's sorrowful, guilt-ridden face as she turned and stepped into her house, carrying a burden she couldn't put into words.

"I've been liking Krystal for so many years. Why does Katie suddenly come into my life?" He asks himself. The question echoes endlessly in his mind. But no matter how hard he tries to make sense of it, no answer comes.

"I'm hurting two people I care about more than anything. How did it come to this? Why does it have to be this way?" he wonders, his heart heavy with confusion and regret.

He twists and turns, searching for a comfortable position, but peace evades him. No matter how he shifts, the weight of his emotions keeps him awake.

— ✦ —

After Katie and Charlie step off the bus, they make their way toward Fraser's house.

The early morning air is cool and still, the park around them quiet except for the rhythm of a basketball hitting the pavement. The sound draws their eyes to the nearby court, where someone is shooting hoops. It's Brandon.

They never would have guessed Brandon lives so close to Fraser's house. His unshaven face and the same rumpled clothes from the night before tell an unmistakable story: he hasn't slept. Alone on the court, he takes shot after shot, but the normally flawless winner of the shootout tournament misses more than half his attempts.

Katie freezes in her tracks, her breath catching at the sight of him. There's a heaviness to the scene that she can't ignore. Her heart aches as she watches him, his movements slower, far less precise than his usual confident style.

Finally, Brandon turns, drawn by the sound of the wheels on the pavement. His gaze lands on the girl with goggles pushing a wheelchair. His eyes meet Katie's, and the world seems to hold its breath. Neither says a word, but neither could look away.

Charlie notices her reaction, glancing between her and Brandon. He opens his mouth as if to say something but stops, unsure of how to break the silence. Meanwhile, the ball bounces off the rim and rolls away, coming to rest on the edge of the court.

Suddenly, Charlie has an idea. Leaning closer to his sister, he whispers, "You go on to Uncle Fraser's house first, sis. I'll stay and shoot some baskets with Brandon, then I'll catch up with you later."

Before Katie can respond, he steps into the line of sight between her and Brandon, breaking their silent connection. He pauses briefly, as if giving her a moment to compose herself, then strides toward the edge of the court to pick up the basketball.

Holding the ball, he looks at Brandon with a small, casual smile. "Mind if I join you?" he asks, his tone light but sincere.

Brandon looks stunned for a moment, his thoughts clearly scattered. He doesn't ask why the siblings are there or where they're heading. Instead, his eyes follow Katie as she wheels herself away, watching her retreating figure in silence.

— ✦ —

When Katie arrives at Fraser's house, Tiffany opens the door with a smile.

"Hi, Katie! Come on in, Mom's waiting for you," she says, guiding Katie toward the family room. As they walk, Tiffany notices Katie is alone and asks, "Is Charlie with you? Daniel loves seeing him."

"He's outside shooting baskets. He'll join us a little later," Katie replies as she wheels herself inside.

"Good morning, Auntie Kelsi," Katie greets warmly as she notices the woman setting cups and plates on the table. "It's been years since I last saw you! You look as young as ever," she adds sincerely.

Kelsi turns around, her face lighting up at the sight of Katie. She immediately walks over and wraps her in a warm embrace.

"Katie, I can't believe you're a high-school senior now! How are your mom and Charlie doing?" Kelsi asks, radiating a warm smile. "Come have some coffee and pastries and we can catch up," she says as she waves Katie over. "Fraser is taking Daniel for a jog and will be back shortly." She adds.

As Tiffany steps out of the room, Katie looks as though she wants to say something but hesitates.

Noticing her unease, Kelsi moves closer and gently places her hands over Katie's. "Katie, we've always considered you part of our family. You can share whatever's on your mind, and we'll do our best to help," she says earnestly, her sincerity evident.

"Thank you, Auntie Kelsi," Katie whispers, her voice tinged with emotion. "You were at the beach yesterday to pick up Tiffany. I guess you must have seen me, Krystal, and Brandon." Her voice softens even further. "I'm sorry I didn't come over to say hello," she adds, a hint of guilt in her tone.

Kelsi nods slightly, her expression calm and encouraging, quietly waiting for Katie to continue.

"Krystal is my best friend at Einstein High, and Brandon is her long-time boyfriend at the same school. He's also the winner of last week's shootout tournament. I…I respect him a lot…" Katie says, her voice faltering, a stark contrast to the confident eloquence she displays during debates.

Kelsi vividly recalls the moment she first saw Krystal and Katie at the beach, both of them radiating a beauty that was hard to ignore. She had also noticed how Brandon's attention was entirely captivated by the two girls, shifting seamlessly between them.

She doesn't need to hear more; her sharp intuition fills in the gaps, piecing together the unspoken dynamics of the situation with quiet understanding.

Meanwhile, outside, Fraser is jogging with Daniel. When Katie called earlier to ask if she could visit, it had caught him by surprise — it wasn't typical for anybody to reach out to visit so early in the morning, especially since he hadn't seen the Santos family in years. Deciding to give Kelsi the chance to learn more from a woman's perspective, Fraser opted to take Daniel out for a jog, planning to meet Katie once Kelsi had spoken with her.

As they jog past the basketball court, Fraser notices two young men sitting on a bench, deep in conversation. One of them is wearing a pair of goggles—goggles

Fraser immediately recognizes as the ones he designed for visually impaired people. It's Charlie. Meanwhile, Daniel spots the other man and excitedly runs over.

"Good morning, Brandon! How's your pretty sister doing? Is she still sad?" Daniel calls out cheerfully, his voice full of youthful innocence.

Brandon looks up, offering a faint smile. "Oh, Daniel, good morning. Krystal is doing okay. But she's my friend, not my sister," he replies softly.

Hearing the little boy mentioning Krystal stirs a sharp ache in Brandon's chest. He forces himself to say she's fine, even though the words feel heavy on his tongue. *How I wish she really was just my sister...* he thinks silently, the weight of unspoken emotions pressing down on him.

Fraser nods at Brandon with a polite smile before turning his attention to Charlie. "Charlie! It's been a while! Look at you! I heard you nearly won a basketball shootout tournament. Glory to our Lord!" he says warmly, giving Charlie a friendly pat on the shoulder.

"Good morning, Uncle Fraser! My sister is at your house now, chatting with Auntie Kelsi," Charlie replies respectfully. "I'll join them a little later. Oh, by the way, this is Brandon Walker, the winner of the shootout tournament. Brandon, meet Uncle Fraser — he's the one who invented the goggles that helped my sister and me gain independence."

119

Brandon's eyes widen in awe as he looks at Fraser, momentarily at a loss for words. "You're Mr. Fraser? The inventor of *Eyes of an Angel*? I've heard so much about you," he says, his voice filled with admiration.

For a brief moment, the distant look in Brandon's eyes transforms into one of genuine respect. Fraser smiles modestly and extends his hand for a firm handshake. "It's a pleasure to meet you, Brandon. I'm glad to see young men like you achieving great things."

~ ~ ~ ~ ~

Chapter 11
An Hour Before Dawn

Fraser and Daniel step into the house just as Katie removes her goggles and wipes the tears from her eyes.

What Fraser sees takes his breath away: a stunning face, framed by lingering traces of tears — so captivating it could soften even the hardest heart, let alone that of a young man. Fraser freezes for a moment, struck by how familiar yet unexpectedly beautiful it is.

This is a face he knows intimately. During countless hours spent programming the helmet and goggles, he had memorized every detail of her features. He had always imagined she would grow into a beauty, but seeing sixteen-year-old Katie now, her radiance still takes him by surprise.

"Daniel, grab a pastry and go play with your sister," Fraser says in a gentle but firm tone, nodding toward the living room. Understanding the cue, Daniel picks up a pastry and scurries off, leaving the adults to talk in private.

Kelsi, having already seen Katie without her goggles at the beach the day before, doesn't appear the least bit surprised. Her calm yet thoughtful gaze shifts from Katie to Fraser.

"Katie has shared her story with me, Fritz," she says softly, her voice carrying a tone of understanding. Katie looks down, avoiding their eyes, her emotions still raw and unspoken.

"Krystal is her best friend at Einstein High and has a long-time boyfriend, Brandon. Yesterday at the beach, something sparked between Katie and Brandon, and Krystal became so jealous that she tried to take her own life by swallowing sleeping pills," Kelsi explains softly, keeping her tone measured and gentle.

"Brandon? The winner of the shootout tournament?" Fraser asks, his mind immediately connecting the dots to the young man he saw outside with Charlie.

Recalling Brandon's disheveled appearance and Charlie's decision to stay outside with him, Fraser quickly pieces the situation together. He also remembers Brandon's earlier comment about Krystal: *"But she's my friend, not my sister."*

The words stir something long buried within Fraser. *"When I first got to know Sarah, did I think of Kelsi the same way?"* His gaze shifts to Kelsi, lingering on her with a thoughtful expression before he nods slightly, lost in his own reflections.

"He wished Krystal were his sister," Fraser muses silently. *"But at that moment, Katie seemed to have overtaken his feelings entirely. Yet, perhaps that's not the whole truth."*

Breaking free from his thoughts, Fraser focuses on Katie and asks, "How long have you known Brandon, Katie?"

"I met Krystal and Brandon last year during the extramural debate competition, Uncle Fraser," Katie answers softly. "After that, I saw them several times during basketball matches between our schools. They were always together."

"You've always been wearing your goggles when you meet them?" Fraser probes further.

"Yes," Katie admits, her tone quiet. "Until yesterday at the beach, when I took them off to catch some sun." She pauses, the memory flashing in her mind — wiping sand from Brandon's face, a moment she can't seem to forget.

Suddenly, Kelsi speaks up. "Krystal is a very beautiful girl, just as lovely as Brit. But yesterday morning, when I saw her, there was a sadness in her eyes. That was likely before you took off your goggles and revealed yourself to Brandon," she says, her tone measured yet clear — the shift in dynamics between Katie and Brandon likely occurred after he saw her face. However, Krystal's stress and melancholy had already been present even before that moment.

"Her parents are going through a divorce," Katie says, her voice heavy with emotion. "She even told me a secret — her dad isn't her biological father. That's why Brandon planned the beach party, to cheer her up, but…" Her voice falters, cracking under the weight of her guilt. "He was paying more attention to me than to her. How did it all go so wrong?"

Fraser studies Katie closely. In his mind's eye, her face shifts, softening into the image of the six-year-old girl she once was — fragile, yet resilient, sitting in her wheelchair, fighting battles far beyond her years.

He makes up his mind. He's going to help her.

Back inside the hospital, Jon and Chelsea walk quietly outside to the lobby. Chelsea glances at Jon, her lips parting as if to speak, but she hesitates. She decides to let him speak first, trusting that whatever he has to say will guide the conversation.

After they settle onto the bench, Jon exhales deeply, running a hand through his hair. "How did Kris end up like this, Chelsea?" he asks, his voice low and pained. Almost as if to himself, he whispers, "Is it because of us? I thought she was strong enough to handle this."

"It's not just us, Jon," Chelsea replies, shaking her head, her tone heavy with concern. "She's been through so much already. And then… she saw Brandon showing affection to Katie." She sighs, her voice softening as she tries to explain.

"Katie?" Jon's brow furrows, his surprise evident. "You mean the girl who always wears goggles and uses a wheelchair? And Brandon… showed more affection to her than Kris?"

"Yes, Katie's her best friend," Chelsea says quietly. "And honestly, without those goggles, Katie's stunning. She has this presence. No young man would fail to notice."

Jon nods slowly, his expression darkening. "So it's not just one thing—it's everything," he murmurs.

Chelsea nods. The silence between them feels thick, filled with an unspoken truth. "Yeah, Jon. All at once." She sighs.

After a moment of silence, Jon says, "I don't know Katie, but I know Brandon well. He's a good kid. And he's genuinely in a relationship with Kris. I'll call him and figure out what's going on."

Chelsea's lips curve into a faint smile, a flicker of relief crossing her face. Jon still cares about Krystal — that much is clear. She looks at him, her eyes shimmering with unspoken gratitude, but she remains silent.

Jon holds her gaze, the silence between them heavy yet charged. Finally, his voice drops to a soft, almost regretful tone. "Chelsea, I'm sorry," he whispers, his hand gently resting on hers.

The words are like music to her ears, striking a chord deep within her. Her eyes brim with tears, threatening to spill over. She swallows hard, her voice trembling as she finally speaks. "Why, Jon… why?"

"It's so foolish of me," Jon begins, his voice barely audible. "Ever since we saw Travis at that restaurant, I haven't been able to stop thinking about it. What if he came back and tried to contact you? What would you do?" He pauses, taking a deep breath as if bracing himself. "And then… I met Samantha."

The mention of Samantha feels like a punch to Chelsea's chest. Her mind flashes back to that morning — seeing Jon with Samantha at the coffee shop. She had been meeting Vanessa, the design manager, to request a custom-made dress for a special occasion. Later, unable to quell her curiosity, she'd asked Vanessa about the commission and learned the truth: Samantha was having a wedding dress custom-designed.

The realization had shaken her to the core. It was then she'd felt her world tilt, unable to focus or stay grounded. She had left the house for a few days to clear her mind, only to be pulled back into chaos by Krystal's incident.

Now, hearing Jon bring up Samantha, the final thread of restraint inside her snaps — but not with anger, only a cold, resigned calm.

"She already has her wedding dress ready. You should go back to her now," Chelsea says, her voice cold and resigned. "I'll take care of Kris from here." She tries to pull her hand away, but Jon holds on tightly.

"This isn't what you think, Chelsea," Jon says firmly. "She's marrying someone else, not me."

Chelsea freezes, her surprise tinged with an unexpected flicker of relief. "So she turned you down, and now you're coming back to me?" she asks, her tone sharp but vulnerable.

Still holding Chelsea's hand, Jon speaks gently, "I admit I acted foolishly. Please, calm down." He moves closer, his tone earnest. "Sammy is a very kind woman, warm and friendly to everyone. I've always seen her as a close friend, and we've shared so much of our stories."

Noticing Chelsea's expression falter, he quickly adds, "But to her, I've always been like a brother — nothing more." Meeting Chelsea's doubtful gaze, he bites his lip and continues, his voice tinged with regret. "I misunderstood her kindness. And that night, when I saw you and Travis looking at each other, something in my mind twisted. It told me that if you ever left me, she'd always be there for me."

Before Chelsea can respond, Jon lowers his eyes, his voice filled with guilt. "I told her that Kris isn't my biological daughter and how much I long to have a child of my own. I also mentioned that you can't conceive again."

Seeing the hurt flicker in Chelsea's eyes, he quickly adds, "I know I shouldn't have shared something so personal. It wasn't my place. But in that moment, I felt like I needed to talk to someone."

"So, she agreed to marry you and gave birth to your child," Chelsea finally responds, her voice calm but laced with pain.

Jon shakes his head and lets out a heavy sigh. "She said she could give me a child, and weeks later, she mentioned wanting to custom-make a wedding dress. Naturally, I took it as a sign she wanted to marry me." He pauses, taking a deep breath before continuing. "Then I found out you were seeing Travis again."

Chelsea exhales shakily, her eyes brimming with tears. "So you've been checking my phone, just looking for an excuse to leave me for Samantha," she whispers, her voice breaking.

"I was wrong — completely wrong." Jon grips Chelsea's hand tightly, as if afraid to let go. "What Sammy meant was to help me have a child through In Vitro Fertilization, not a real marriage. She already has someone she plans to marry."

Chelsea stares at him, stunned. *In Vitro Fertilization to give a friend a child? What kind of friendship is this?* Her perception of Samantha shifts drastically—from a selfish woman who destroyed another's family to an admirable one, selfless and kind beyond measure.

"What? Is it possible?" Her mouth opens wide, her eyes even wider. "Why didn't you tell me earlier?"

"I...I just found out the day before." Jon lowers his eyes. "That day after you left the coffee shop, she asked me why you seemed so upset, so I told her about us. She immediately explained this to me and told me to ask you back."

"Then why don't you?" Chelsea starts to calm down a bit.

"I'm...I'm afraid to." Jon bites his lips. "I know You are seeing Travis again."

Before Chelsea can rebuke, what Jon says next really surprises her.

129

"Do you know who I was with last night when you called?" he asks, a faint smile playing on his lips as he looks at her. "It was your Travis."

Chelsea, her eyes still brimming with tears, is utterly speechless.

"I don't know how he found me," Jon continues. "But he explained everything about that night. He told me he was saying goodbye to you for good, and that kiss was his way of closing the chapter. He's leaving to become a missionary pastor and is moving to Asia."

Chelsea's voice rises, calmer now but still edged with frustration. "But I've explained this to you already, and you wouldn't listen!"

"Yes, my fault, Chelsea," Jon replies, reaching out his other hand to hold hers. His tone softens. "But Travis told me something that really touched my heart — he knew Kris is his real daughter, yet he chose to let go and stay away. He said he didn't want to disrupt her life because she sees me as her daddy, and she always will."

Chelsea can't hold back any longer. She pulls her hands away from Jon's and wraps her arms around his neck. Their lips meet in a tender, tearful kiss, while tears stream down both of their cheeks, mingling with the overwhelming emotions of regret, forgiveness, and love.

Just then, Krystal steps out of the patient room and into the lobby. The sight before her — the two people she loves most locked in a tearful embrace — calms the turmoil in her heart, like Jesus calming the storm. Overwhelmed with relief and joy, she rushes toward her parents, throwing her arms around them and hugging them tightly, tears of joy streaming down her face.

— ✦ —

After chatting with Charlie and meeting Fraser, Brandon finally returns home, his thoughts swirling. Despite Charlie being only fourteen, his words linger in Brandon's mind, striking a deep chord.

"My sister likes you a lot, and so does Krystal. I pray you can make the right choice," Charlie had said, his youthful sincerity carrying a weight that Brandon couldn't ignore.

Sitting in the quiet of his home, Brandon reflects on Charlie's words, feeling lost and uncertain.

Suddenly, a thought strikes him — Charlie and Katie had sought advice from Fraser. Though his encounter with Fraser was brief, Brandon couldn't help but sense the man's kindness and wisdom.

"If he can create 'Eyes of an Angel' to help so many people, he must be capable of helping Katie out of this situation," Brandon tells himself, a flicker of determination beginning to form amidst his confusion.

Then, his thoughts shift to Krystal. *"I wonder how she's doing now. Katie's not around. Maybe I should drop by and see Auntie Chelsea too."* With that, he gets up and heads to his car.

When he arrives at the hospital, the nurse at the registration desk informs him that Krystal has already been discharged.

"Early this morning she couldn't recognize anything or anyone, but just a few hours later, she's fine to be checked out?" The thought lingers uneasily in his mind as he drives to Krystal's house.

Once there, he parks outside and sits in his car, staring at the front door. Memories flood back — it was only last night that he stood there, but not alone; Katie was with him.

As he watches, Krystal's front door seems to blur and morph into Katie's front door. In his mind, he pictures Katie's back as she grips her crutches, hobbling slowly inside the house.

"What is she thinking now?" The question echoes in his mind, relentless and unshakable.

~ ~ ~ ~ ~

Chapter 12
Even Angels Need Guidance

Katie and Charlie sit quietly in their house, both lost in thought. The silence stretches until Charlie speaks, his voice breaking the stillness.

"Sis, while you were talking with Uncle Fraser, I had a chance to chat with Auntie Kelsi," he begins, "She shared her story with me about how she met Uncle Fraser."

Katie lifts her head and looks at him, curious. She knows Charlie, reserved by nature, wouldn't bring something up unless it matters to him. "What did she tell you?" she asks gently.

Charlie hesitates for a moment, searching for the right words. "She said that when she first met Uncle Fraser, she wasn't a Christian. But after getting to know him, she started going to church with him because... well, because she liked him a lot."

Katie's eyebrows lift slightly, but before she can respond, Charlie continues. "Auntie Kelsi said that when she loves someone, she's willing to change parts of herself to spend more time with him."

Katie studies her brother, sensing there's more on his mind than just retelling the story.

"…Amanda asked me to teach her how to shoot baskets," Charlie continues, his voice barely above a whisper. "She knows how much I love playing basketball… but she's never played sports before."

Katie's smile softens, and she gently pats his shoulder. "Amanda is such a sweet girl. I'm so happy she likes you, Charlie."

Her words hang warmly in the air, but as her gaze drifts, the smile on her face slowly fades. Thoughts of Brandon creep into her mind.

But what Charlie says next catches Katie off guard, touching her deeply.

"Auntie Kelsi wasn't just talking about herself," he says softly, his voice steady despite the weight of his words. "She was talking about you, Sis. She meant… in order to figure out how you really feel about Brandon, are you willing to make changes for him?"

Charlie hesitates, his gaze dropping to the floor, but he presses on. "That's what she wanted me to tell you."

Katie freezes, her heart skipping a beat as his words sink in. She looks at her younger brother, seeing the courage it took for him to say something so personal. The room feels still, save for the faint echo of the question lingering between them.

She knows she's always been independent, assertive, and decisive—qualities that have made her a natural leader of the debate team, something she takes great pride in. Deep down, she senses that these are the very traits that attract Brandon to her.

"Why would I change myself for him?" she asks herself, the question lingering as her thoughts swirl.

After a long pause she speaks, her voice quiet and reflective. "I talked with Uncle Fraser for a while. He told me something that stayed with me even now." Her words falter slightly as tears begin to well in her eyes.

"He said that as I was slowly regaining my speech, one of the first questions I asked him was, 'Why would God let something like this happen to our family?'" Katie reaches for a tissue, dabbing at her eyes before continuing.

"He told me that God allows things to happen for a reason. That He let you and me face our disabilities, but He also created him to invent *Eyes of an Angel* to help people like us. He said he liked Auntie Sarah a lot, but he came to realize that God brought her into his life so he could meet and help our family. His true love, though, has always been Auntie Kelsi."

Katie's voice, though thick with emotion, carries a steady sense of hope. "He told me God is using us for a bigger purpose, that He's pleased with what we've become. There will be times we have to make hard decisions, but if we choose wisely, the outcome will always be better than we can imagine."

She exhales deeply, her words trailing into the stillness of the room, as though the weight of them has finally lifted from her shoulders.

That evening, Katie lies in her bed, gently holding a pink heart pendant, its smooth surface warming against her palm.

"Am I the Sarah or the Kelsi in Brandon's heart?" she wonders, the question swirling in her mind. *"Krystal has known Brandon for years. Did I appear in his life just to serve a particular purpose for them?"*

As doubt begins to creep in, Fraser's words echo in her thoughts, wrapping her in a quiet sense of comfort.

"You and Charlie are angels to me," he had said. *"Without you, I wouldn't have found the inspiration to create Eyes of an Angel. And without its success, I wouldn't have been able to save Kelsi's brother Pat from a stroke."* Then, with a

playful grin, he added, *"And if I hadn't saved Pat, Kelsi might not have married me."*

Katie's lips lift into a soft smile, the warmth of the memory easing the heaviness in her heart. Fraser's words, full of gratitude and purpose, fill the room with a quiet hope, reminding her that every connection has its own meaning and value.

She recalls how, just before she left, Uncle Fraser had briefly excused himself, returning from his office with a heart-shaped pendant in hand. Holding it out to her, he said, "Each of us is an angel to somebody — someone you may not even realize. Every decision we make can change another person's life. If you have the heart of an angel, you'll always strive to make the right decision."

"This *'Heart of an Angel'* is something I created some time ago," he continued, placing the pendant gently in her palm. "When you press it with a finger from each hand and focus on your issue, it will read and analyze your situation. It's designed to inspire you with the right decision."

Katie looks at the pendant now, its smooth surface gleaming faintly in the soft light of her room. Fraser's words linger in her mind, filling her with a sense of purpose and hope.

— ✦ —

The next morning, Katie and Charlie take the bus to school as usual. The day passes quickly, and as the final bell rings, Charlie approaches his sister, his cheeks tinged with a hint of nervousness.

"Sis," he says shyly, "I'm going to teach Amanda how to shoot baskets. We'll come home later."

Katie smiles warmly at him, her eyes filled with encouragement. "Sure, Charlie. Have fun, and I'll see you tonight."

With that, she wheels herself toward the bus stop as she usually does — this time, without Charlie by her side. The quiet solitude feels different, but her smile lingers, proud of her brother's growing confidence.

She recalls the text message she received from Brandon earlier that morning. He had written that he wanted to see her after school and talk. If she had received it yesterday, she would have felt confused and unsure. Now, she hasn't yet responded, still weighing what to say and do.

As she waits at the bus stop, her thoughts are interrupted by a familiar figure approaching. It's Jake, the towering Goliath who had harassed her and Charlie in the school gym, wearing his trademark smirk. This time, however, her David isn't by her side.

"Hi, my princess," Jake says mockingly, stopping a few feet away. "Alone today? Charlie boy isn't here to protect you?"

Katie sighs deeply, her patience already wearing thin. "No, not again," she mutters under her breath. She meets his gaze steadily, refusing to show fear. "Please, just leave me alone. I'm not in the mood for this."

Jake's smirk widens as he places his hands on the handles of her wheelchair. "Apologize to me, or I'll push over your carriage!" he taunts, loud enough for the crowd at the bus stop to hear.

Before Katie can respond, a voice cuts through the air behind her, firm and unmistakable. "Leave her alone, Jake!"

Katie freezes, startled. She can't turn to see who it is, but the voice is familiar — and unexpected. It's Brock.

"Hey Brock, stay out of this! This is between her and me!" Jake snaps, stepping back instinctively. He knows Brock is a better streetfighter — a fact that he once exploited to persuade him to help harass Charlie and Katie at Uncle Leo's pizzeria.

But Brock steps forward, his stance firm and unyielding. "Just leave, Jake. You shouldn't be bothering her. She's... she's my friend."

Jake bursts into laughter. "Your friend? Oh, I see. You like her, huh? You like this funny-looking gal in a wheelchair? Fine, Brock, she's all yours." With a dismissive wave, Jake turns and strides away.

As the tension eases, Brock steps around to face Katie. His expression softens, and his voice is quieter than she's ever heard it. "I'm sorry I said you're my friend," he murmurs, a sharp contrast to the rough, confrontational tone she remembers. "I only said that so he'd leave you alone."

Katie blinks, caught off guard. Brock seems… different. The defiant, brash persona she had come to expect from him is gone. In its place is a hint of vulnerability, a sincerity she never thought she'd see in him.

Fraser's words echo in her mind: *"Each of us is an angel to somebody — someone you may not even realize. Every decision we make can change another person's life."*

Did I become his angel? She wonders, the thought surprised her. The weight of the encounter begins to lift, leaving her heart unexpectedly lighter.

Without thinking, she blurts out, "You are my friend, Brock. And… thanks." Extending her hand toward him, she offers a gesture of trust.

Brock hesitates, his eyes flickering with uncertainty, but finally extends his hand to clasp hers. Their handshake lingers briefly, and the quiet moment is interrupted by a few kids in the crowd starting to clap. The applause quickly spread, rippling through the onlookers. Brock gives a shy nod, his face slightly flushed, then turns and walks away without a word.

Katie looks around at the clapping crowd and smiles faintly, her expression calm yet thoughtful. She thinks about Brandon.

She pulls out her phone and types a message to Brandon:

"Meet me at Leo's pizzeria in half an hour."

She reasons it's better than meeting him at her house, especially in case Charlie comes back early. Deep down, though, she wonders if part of her choice is to see how Brandon handles himself in the notoriously unfriendly environment of Leo's pizzeria, to protect her as the way Charlie does when being bullied.

Though she prides herself on her strength and independence, a quiet truth lingers beneath it all — she yearns for care and protection. After all, she is still just a girl.

Leo's pizzeria isn't far from the bus stop, and as Katie wheels her way there, her mind races with questions. *I told him we should cool off for a while. Why is he reaching out now? And why did I agree to see him? Does he like me more than Krystal? How is Krystal even feeling about all this? What's going to happen to our friendship?*

Her thoughts swirl as she approaches the intersection and notices Brandon standing across the street in front of Leo's. He waves at her, a warm smile lighting up his face. It's been only a day, but to them, it seems they haven't seen each other in ages.

Without thinking, Katie wheels herself toward him, crossing the intersection just as the light turns amber. She's so focused on reaching him that she doesn't notice a sedan is barreling through the red light.

"Katie, watch out!" Brandon's yell cuts through the air.

Before she can react, she feels a sudden, forceful push from behind. Her wheelchair narrowly avoids the speeding car, but she's thrown from her seat, tumbling to the ground. The sound of screeching tires is followed by a pained yell — a voice she recognizes immediately.

It's Brock.

The world blurs around her, and as the adrenaline fades, darkness creeps in. His yell is the last thing she hears before everything goes black.

~ ~ ~ ~ ~

Chapter 13
Human Side of an Angel

When Katie regains consciousness, she finds herself lying in an unfamiliar bed, an IV strapped to her arm. Her goggles are on the table next to her. The soft hum of hospital machines fills the room, and a nurse is typing notes beside her.

"What happened?" Katie asks, her voice weak but steady.

The nurse turns to her with a reassuring smile. "You were almost hit by a car. You fell from your wheelchair and were in shock, but physically, you're okay. You should feel better in a few hours. We've notified your family — they're on their way."

Katie nods faintly, processing the nurse's words. As the nurse steps out of the room, she closes her eyes and tries to piece together the fragments of her memory.

I saw Brandon waving, and I crossed the street... then I heard him yell. Someone pushed my wheelchair from behind, and I barely missed the car. But... but I heard Brock cry out.

Her eyes snap open, her heart pounding. *Brock saved me! But... is he okay?*

The events play back in her mind, slowly assembling piece by piece, as worry grips her chest.

"It must have been Brandon who brought me here. But... where is he?" Katie wonders, a pang of disappointment flickering through her as she scans the empty room.

Feeling too weak to move, call Charlie, or even find out what happened to Brock, she reaches for the pink heart pendant Fraser had given her. Holding it gently, she focuses her thoughts on Brandon, Krystal, and Brock, hoping for clarity.

With both hands, she squeezes the heart. It lights up, blinking in a soothing rhythm, cycling silently through a rainbow of colors.

As the soft, radiant glow reflects in her eyes, her swirling thoughts begin to settle. The tension in her chest eases, and a quiet sense of calm washes over her, as if the heart were gently guiding her emotions back into balance.

Katie closes her eyes, letting the soft rhythm of the pendant's light steady her thoughts. Her mind drifts to Krystal. *"She's my best friend, and she's going through so much right now. I wish Brandon is with her, comforting her."* It's the first thought that surfaces, simple and heartfelt.

Then her mind shifts to the moments just before the accident. *"Brandon was only a few steps away when he saw the car. He yelled to warn me. But Brock... Brock must have been further away, on the other side of the street. Yet he ran, without hesitation, and pushed me out of harm's way without even saying a word."*

The thought lingers, unsettling her. *Why would he do that? What made him risk himself so completely?* For reasons she can't quite explain, it bothers her—nagging at her like a question she's not ready to answer.

The door creaks open, and Katie looks up to see Charlie and Amanda stepping in. Concern is written all over Charlie's face as he rushes to her side.

"Brandon called and said you almost got run over in front of Uncle Leo's shop. What happened?" he asks urgently.

"I'm okay," Katie replies, her voice calm but weary. "Somebody pushed my wheelchair just in time to miss the hit. I just need some rest." She keeps her explanation brief, unsure how much to share.

145

Before Charlie can press her further, Amanda steps forward, her eyes soft with worry. "When we heard you had an accident, Charlie and I were so worried. I'm so glad you're okay, Sis Katie." She leans down and wraps Katie in a warm embrace.

"Get some rest, and we'll talk later," Amanda says with a kind smile before pulling back.

Katie nods, grateful for their presence but feeling the weight of unanswered questions still lingering in her mind.

Just moments after Charlie and Amanda leave, the door creaks open again. Brandon steps in, carrying a bouquet of red roses, a box of Lady Godiva chocolates, and a bright red Squishmallow. His expression is a mix of anticipation and nervous energy.

Once inside, he places everything carefully on the bed and strides towards Katie, enveloping her in an embrace he's clearly longed to give but had restrained himself until now.

"Hi, Katie," he says softly, his voice tinged with both relief and concern. "How are you feeling? I was terrified when I saw that car almost hit you." His gaze locks onto hers, filled with sincerity and unspoken emotion.

Katie manages a faint smile. "I'm fine, just a little shaken," she replies, her voice steady but distant. She had expected her heart to leap with excitement at the sight of him, yet inexplicably, the emotion she anticipated just isn't there.

Katie's gaze shifts to the gifts Brandon brought, and she forces a faint smile. "You shouldn't have," she says quietly, her tone betraying a hint of hesitation. As the silence lingers, her thoughts start to spiral.

Red... that's Krystal's favorite color. Does he even remember I always wear yellow — the gym, the beach, everywhere? And chocolates? Krystal loves Lady Godiva, but I've never been one for candy. Does he even see me? In his mind, I'm Krystal.

Her arms instinctively tighten around the Squishmallow as Brandon gently places it in her lap, a gesture she knows is meant to comfort her. *He went through so much trouble — bringing me flowers, candy, and a toy — but...* she thinks, *all I really wanted was for him to be there when I opened my eyes, to truly see me. But he wasn't. And even now... he still doesn't understand.*

Brandon, seemingly unaware of the storm brewing in her mind, busies himself placing the roses in a vase beside her bed. The gesture feels hollow to Katie, like he's completing a checklist instead of truly seeing her.

Katie watches him quietly, her emotions swirling. After a pause, she asks, her voice barely above a whisper, "Brandon, how's Krystal? Did you see her today? Have you had a chance to explain to her?"

She's unsure if the exhaustion she feels is purely physical or if it stems from the uncertainty and emotions weighing on her.

Brandon shakes his head. "She didn't come to school today, but she was discharged yesterday afternoon. So the doctor must think she's doing fine and didn't need to stay in the hospital."

Katie's brow furrows slightly. "But did you go to her house to see her?" she presses, her tone firm despite her weariness.

"I… I did drop by her house," Brandon admits, hesitating as he feels her gaze lock onto him. "But I didn't ring the bell."

"Why not?" Katie asks, her eyes searching his face, her voice softer now but no less insistent.

Brandon stammers briefly, then takes a deep breath. "I… I was thinking about you," he finally confesses, his voice trembling as he meets her eyes.

Katie falls silent. The words hang in the air, heavy and charged. This is the answer she longs to hear — but also the one she dreads.

"He cares about me more than about her. How can it be? Why?" she asks herself, the questions swirling in her mind with no clear answers. Her emotions churn, a

mixture of joy, confusion, and guilt, leaving her unable to respond.

Brandon moves closer and rests his hand gently on hers. Katie pulls her hand away almost immediately.

"Let's cool off for a while, Brandon," Katie says, her voice steady but sincere. "You should spend more time with Krystal. She needs you the most right now, especially with everything going on in her family. You're the only one she can truly turn to."

She pauses, taking a deep breath before summoning the courage to continue. "I like you, Brandon. I really do. But... she needs you a lot more than I do." Her voice trembles slightly as tears begin to well in her eyes.

"She's our dearest friend, and we can't hurt her like this," Katie says, her voice breaking slightly as she turns her head to hide the tears welling in her eyes. The room falls into a heavy silence, her words hanging in the air like an unspoken plea.

Brandon remains silent, her words echoing in his mind. *"We can't hurt her like this..."* he murmurs to himself, the weight of the truth sinking in. Finally, he nods, forcing a faint smile. Without another word, he leans in for a light, hesitant embrace before turning and walking out of the room.

As the door closes behind him, the composure Katie fought so hard to maintain crumbles. Tears stream down her face, silent and unrelenting, as she clutches the pink heart pendant tightly in her hand.

Moments later, the nurse enters the room with a simple dinner tray and Katie's wheelchair.

"Miss Santos, you're discharged," the nurse says with a warm smile. "Please have your dinner, and you'll be ready to go home."

Katie nods, glancing at the tray as she uncovers her meal. Suddenly, a thought strikes her, and she looks up at the nurse.

"During the car accident... was there a man near my wheelchair? Was he also hit by the car?" she asks politely.

The nurse's expression softens. "Oh, Mr. Tyler? Is he the one who pushed your wheelchair out of the way?"

Katie's breath catches. "Yes... that's him."

The nurse nods gently. "He reacted very quickly, but the car still hit him at the left leg. Fortunately, it's not very serious, and the surgery was successful. He's resting in room 14, five doors down on the left."

Katie sits back, relief and worry mingling in her chest as she processes the news. *Brock...* she thinks, the memory of his selfless act replaying in her mind.

After finishing her light dinner, Katie wheels herself down the corridor to room 14. She knocks gently and pushes the door open, finding Brock lying in bed. His left leg is in a cast, suspended in a stand, and his face is partially bandaged.

As she enters, Brock's eyes flutter open. "Are you okay?" he asks immediately, his voice laced with concern. "I heard you scream. I hope the car didn't hit you."

Katie shakes her head, her voice soft. "The car didn't hit me; I just got thrown off from my wheelchair." Her gaze lingers on Brock's injured face, taking in the bandages and the cast. *"He only worries about me, not about himself..."* she thinks, her heart tightening.

"Thank you for saving my life, Brock," she says, her voice trembling as tears begin to well up, unable to hold back the emotion she feels.

Brock responds with a bright smile, his usual mischievous glint still present despite the pain. "I only did what I needed to do." Then, with a playful smirk, he adds, "You told me to get a life, stop causing trouble. Guess this counts as my first good deed."

Katie can't help but smile through her tears, but before she can reply, Brock suddenly asks, "You know my name is Brock, but… I don't even know yours."

His words strike a chord deep within her. *He doesn't even know my name, and he risked his life for me?* The thought sends a fresh wave of emotion crashing over her, and tears stream down her face. Without her goggles, her teary eyes glisten under the soft hospital light.

Brock, seeing her tears and her unmasked, vulnerable expression, is momentarily stunned. He stares at her, speechless, as if seeing her for the first time. "You're… beautiful," he says quietly, the words slipping out before he can stop them.

Over the past few days, Katie has seen the impact her unmasked appearance has had on others. She's surprised quite a few people: Brock, Krystal, Chip, Brandon, Auntie Chelsea, and even Auntie Kelsi and Uncle Fraser. But this time, the reaction comes from someone who is risking his life for her.

"I'm Katie, Brock," she says softly, placing her hand over his. "Why… how did you come just in time to save me?" The question has been nagging at her ever since she woke up in the hospital.

"I saw you leave the bus stop and head this way," Brock replies, his eyes dropping to avoid hers. "This is a rough neighborhood, and no girl should walk here alone… and, uh, I was thinking about grabbing a pizza here…"

His last statement barely holds water, but Katie doesn't need him to spell it out. She understands. He had followed her to protect her, even if he couldn't bring himself to admit it.

She is speechless for a moment. She doesn't know what to say. Her tears keep streaming down.

Finally, she places her other hand gently over his and whispers, "Thanks again, Brock." Then, without waiting for a reply, she withdraws her hands and wheels herself out of the room.

Brock watches as she disappears down the hallway. He's never been one to wear his emotions on his sleeve, and he hadn't expected her to come see him at all. But she did.

When she came to see him, he didn't find the assertive, no-nonsense girl who once told him to "get a life." Instead, he saw someone tender, vulnerable — a girl who shed tears for him.

A sudden urge swells within him, a deep desire to pull her into his arms and wipe away those tears. But the reality of his injured foot, suspended on a stand, keeps him rooted to his bed, unable to act.

In the lobby, Charlie and Amanda wait patiently for Katie.

They've seen Brandon come and go, and when Katie emerges, they notice the streaks of tears on her face. What they don't realize, though, is that those tears weren't for Brandon—they were for someone else.

Charlie, having already shared his sister's story with Amanda, meets her gaze with a quiet, knowing look. Without exchanging a word, the two fall into step beside Katie, walking her out in thoughtful silence.

~ ~ ~ ~ ~

Chapter 14
Invitation, Wheelchair, and Crutches

Brandon sits in his car, parked at a distance from the hospital entrance, his eyes fixed on Katie as she walks out with Charlie and Amanda. He's been waiting for her for some time, but the sight of her with them makes him hesitate.

Just then, his phone rings, breaking his focus. He glances at the screen. It's Jon Perkins — Krystal's dad. Of all people, he's the last person Brandon expected to hear from.

That evening, the two of them meet at a quiet coffee shop. The air feels heavy with unspoken tension as they sit down.

"Brandon," Jon begins, wasting no time. His tone is steady but carries a hint of concern. "Can you tell me what happened between you and Kris? She's been so upset lately... and she's not talking to anyone."

"Uh, actually, I'm not really sure, Uncle," Brandon says, hesitating as he tries to piece together a response, even though he'd anticipated Jon might ask this question. "Maybe it was last Saturday at the beach party. There were some bullies who came over, and she seemed pretty shaken."

He knows the explanation sounds weak, even to his own ears, but he's stalling, hoping Jon will reveal more.

"Be honest with me, Brandon," Jon says, his tone sincere. "You're a good boy, and our whole family likes you. We all see how well you've been looking out for Kris, and we really appreciate it." Jon meets Brandon's eyes, his gaze steady as he adds, "But tell me the truth — is this about Katie?

The question lands heavily, and for a moment, Brandon freezes. "I..." he begins, but his voice falters. He looks away, exhaling sharply through his nose. "It's not like that."

His words are weak, and his expression betrays him, a flicker of guilt flashing across his face. It's clear he's not ready to admit the truth, even though it's written all over him.

Jon watches him for a moment, his eyes narrowing slightly, but he doesn't press. Instead, his own thoughts begin to swirl, unbidden. Samantha. Chelsea. The choices he made, the lines he crossed, the regrets he still carries. The weight of it settles on him like a familiar shadow.

With a deep sigh, Jon breaks the silence. "I understand," he says quietly. "I'm a man too, Brandon. I've made my share of mistakes — mistakes I still regret. But you..." He pauses, meeting Brandon's gaze with a sharp intensity. "You have a chance to do better. Don't let yourself become the man who looks back and wishes he'd handled things differently. It's not worth it."

The words hang in the air, heavy and charged, as Brandon swallows hard. There's no lecture in Jon's tone, no judgment — just the hard-earned wisdom of someone who's been there.

Both of them fall silent, the weight of Jon's words lingering in the air. Brandon chews on them thoughtfully.

Suddenly, a spark flashes in his thoughts, and he ventures to ask a question that's been gnawing at him.

"Uncle," Brandon begins hesitantly, "how is Kris now? Last time I... saw her in the hospital, she had temporary amnesia. She couldn't recognize anything."

Jon's face softens, and a small smile touches his lips. "Ever since I came back home, she's recovered, Brandon," he replies. After a brief pause, he adds, "I made a mistake by leaving the woman I truly loved, and I don't want to see you doing the same."

Brandon's heart skips a beat at Jon's words. They strike deeper than he expected, resonating in a way he's not ready to admit.

"She'll be back at school tomorrow," Jon says with a reassuring smile, patting Brandon on the shoulder. "Take the time to talk with her, to comfort her."

Brandon nods, the weight of Jon's advice settling over him. These are the last words exchanged before they part ways outside the coffee shop, leaving Brandon alone with his thoughts — and the realization of what he must do.

— ✦ —

Back at Katie's house, the air is still, with only the faint hum of a clock filling the quiet space. She sits on the couch with Charlie after Amanda has left. Looks like Charlie's about to say something, but Katie beats him to it.

"I was on my way to meet Brandon at Uncle Leo's," she begins, her voice carrying an edge of lingering disbelief. "And a car almost hit me. If it hadn't been for someone pushing my car out of the way just in time, I'd have been run over."

Charlie's mouth opens, ready to speak, but Katie doesn't let him. "Do you know who my guardian angel was?" she says, her voice rising slightly. "It was Brock! Remember? The guy you knocked down at Uncle Leo's that night?"

"What?" Charlie's jaw drops. "Brock? *He* saved you, Sis?"

Katie nods, her expression softening as she recalls the moment. "Yeah, Charlie. The same Brock. Turns out, there's more to him than we thought."

Charlie leans back, still processing the revelation, and mutters, "Well, I'll be darned... But why was he there when you were meeting Brandon? Could it really just be a coincidence?"

Katie hesitates, then decides not to hide the truth. "Actually, I met him at the bus stop this afternoon," she says softly, her voice carrying a hint of fondness. "Big Jake came and harassed me, and Brock stepped in. He told Jake to leave me alone because... because I'm his friend."

A slight blush rises to her cheeks as she repeats the words, savoring them a little more each time.

Noticing the change in Katie's tone when she mentions Brock, Charlie smirks and teases, "Seems like you're hiding something from me, Sis."

Katie hesitates, her cheeks warming, but she knows there's no point in denying it. "Actually," she starts quietly, "it happened last week when you took Amanda out for pizza."

She takes a breath, then begins to recount the story — how Brock came to her, stripped off her goggles, and how he eventually walked away.

After she finishes, Katie adds softly, "He must come to this stop often, but I've hardly noticed him."

Noticing the faint smile on her lips and the glimmer in her eyes, Charlie suddenly says, "It's not a coincidence... for Brock to save you, I mean."

"Oh, what do you mean, Charlie?" Katie asks, feigning surprise, though deep down, she feels the same.

"Brock likes you, Sis," Charlie says shyly. "Ever since the first time he saw your face, he's been coming to see you every day. It's not just chance."

Katie's eyes widen slightly, her heart skipping a beat. Charlie continues, his own face reddening. "I know because... I feel the same way about Amanda. I want to see her every day too."

What Charlie says next touches Katie's heart even more. "He doesn't want you to see him," Charlie says softly. "He just wants to quietly protect you when you need it."

Katie's breath catches, the words sinking in deeply. For a moment, she's silent, her thoughts swirling with a mixture of warmth and wonder.

— ✦ —

The next morning at Einstein High, Brandon waits anxiously in the school parking lot. His heart races as he spots Chelsea's car pulling in. Moments later, Krystal steps out slowly, looking around hesitantly.

Without a second thought, Brandon rushes over, extending a hand to her. Krystal freezes for a moment, unsure, and glances back at Chelsea. Chelsea gives her a warm smile and a subtle nod of encouragement.

Feeling reassured, Krystal takes Brandon's hand. Together, they walk slowly toward the classrooms, her steps growing steadier with each one.

"You worried me to death, Kris," Brandon says earnestly. It's the truth, though it's the same thing he's said to Katie before.

"Really?" Krystal chuckles softly, a hint of teasing in her voice. "Then why didn't you come to see me?"

Brandon hesitates for a split second before responding, "I tried to, but I heard you were already out of the hospital. And... Katie almost got hit by a car yesterday and ended up in the hospital."

His answer comes quickly, but his tone lacks conviction. Even though Krystal isn't entirely convinced, the mention of her best friend being hospitalized shifts her focus to concern.

"Katie almost had an accident? What happened?" she asks, her voice laced with worry. "Is she out today? Is she hurt?"

"She was discharged yesterday evening," Brandon replies. "Apparently, someone pushed her wheelchair away just in time to save her. She's just shaken up but otherwise okay."

Hearing the two best friends ask about each other's well-being so naturally touches Brandon deeply. For a moment, he simply watches, reminded of how much they mean to each other — and to him.

During recess, they meet again in the schoolyard, sitting side by side on a bench. The late morning sun filters through the trees, casting dappled shadows around them.

"Brandon, I'm okay now," Krystal begins, her tone light but sincere. "My parents are getting back together... Why don't you look surprised?" She tilts her head, studying him.

Brandon smiles warmly. "Kris, your dad told me last night. I already knew the great news. I'm so happy for you."

Without hesitation, he moves closer, wrapping his arms around her. Unlike Katie's reserved nature, Krystal returns the embrace with unrestrained joy, resting her head on his shoulder as they've done countless times before.

In that moment, Brandon feels the familiar warmth that only she can bring — a feeling so uniquely hers that it stirs something deep within him, something no one else could replicate.

He looks down at her, meeting her gentle gaze. Taking a deep breath, he says softly, "Kris, I'm sorry." He stops, the words catching in his throat. He doesn't know what else to say.

Krystal responds with a sweet smile. She lifts her hand and presses her index finger lightly against his lips — a simple, tender gesture that could melt any men's heart.

"I understand," she whispers, her voice as warm and reassuring as her touch.

That evening, Katie and Charlie visit the hospital, hoping to see Brock, but are disappointed to learn he was discharged just moments earlier.

"I don't have his contact information. How am I supposed to thank him?" Katie says, half to Charlie, half to herself, her tone tinged with frustration.

Noticing the rare look of disappointment in her eyes, Charlie grins and says, "Sis, give it a week or so. He'll find you at the bus stop." With a playful smirk, he adds, "Then you can thank him however you like."

Katie gently punches Charlie on the shoulder, but her smile betrays her amusement. Despite herself, she feels a spark of hope at his words.

A couple of days later, Katie receives a text from Krystal, inviting her over for dinner. The message is brief but heartfelt, describing it as a dinner of gratitude and appreciation.

"What are they thanking me for?" Katie wonders, her thoughts swirling. "She knows I almost took Brandon away from her, and she's thankful? It doesn't make sense."

As she questions it, the events of that day replay slowly in her mind. She recalls running into Jake and Brock first, long before agreeing to meet Brandon. Back then, she cared so deeply for Brandon that she completely overlooked Krystal.

Then came the near accident. She remembers how it should have been easier for Brandon to save her, but it wasn't—it was Brock who pushed her out of harm's way.

In the hospital, clutching the angel pendant she wore, Katie had prayed in her confusion. Something shifted in her heart during that quiet moment. She realized that Krystal, not her, was the one Brandon was meant to be with. Brandon should be by Krystal's side, caring for her as he always had.

Then there's Brock — a guy who risked his life to save her, even though she had once told him to "get a life," a guy who didn't even know her name. As the pieces fall into place, she realizes he had quietly followed her, not to intrude, but to protect her from the shadows.

What she doesn't yet fully grasp is that, without even trying, Brock is quietly stealing her heart from Brandon.

She grasps the heart pendant tightly, her fingers trembling as tears well in her eyes. Uncle Fraser's departing words echo in her mind:

"Each of us is an angel to somebody—someone you may not even realize. Every decision we make can

change another person's life. If you have the heart of an
angel, you'll always strive to make the right decision."

The weight of his wisdom settles over her, filling her with both clarity and emotion. She knows now what she must do, and for the first time, the choice feels peaceful.

~ ~ ~ ~ ~

Chapter 15
The Heart of an Angel

The day before the invitation dinner, Katie and Charlie wait at the bus stop after school.

Suddenly, Charlie leans in and whispers, "Brock is a block away behind us."

Katie quickly turns, spotting a figure on crutches trying to move out of sight. But with his injury, he's not fast enough to escape. Without hesitation, Katie wheels herself toward him, Charlie following close behind.

"Hey, Brock, don't run! I want to see you!" Katie calls out, her voice loud and clear.

Brock stops in his tracks and sighs, turning back with a playful grin. "I can't run," he says, gesturing to his crutches. "See these?"

Then, his gaze shifts to Charlie, and he chuckles nervously. "Charlie, don't hit me! I'm your sister's friend!"

Charlie smirks, shaking his head, while Katie's determined expression softens into a smile.

When they reach him, Katie's eyes fall on Brock's cast. Her unspoken gaze carries more emotion than any words could convey.

"Oh, it's just one leg," Brock says with a teasing grin, noticing her concern. "I've got another one!" His attempt to lighten the mood brings a faint smile to her lips.

Charlie steps forward, his tone sincere. "Brock, thanks for saving my sister. And... I'm sorry I punched you the other day."

Brock chuckles, shifting his crutches to free a hand and pat Charlie on the shoulder. "You punched away my old self, pal."

Then, turning his grin toward Katie, he adds, "And she told me to get a life. Still working on that one." His playful remark brings a soft laugh from Katie, her earlier tension easing as the three of them share the moment.

Suddenly, Katie gathers her courage and blurts out, "Tomorrow, we got invited to a dinner, and I'd like you to come with us." She pauses, and adds firmly, "I insist."

Brock's heart skips a beat. *She's inviting me to a dinner? With her? I must be dreaming...* But then her last words snap him back to reality.

"I'm not dreaming," he murmurs, glancing down at his crutches. With a small smile, he says, "But how can I come with these?"

Katie doesn't miss a beat. "I have my wheelchair, and you have your crutches—that's a perfect pair..." She trails off, realizing her slip of the tongue. Her cheeks flush a deep pink.

Brock stares at her for a moment, his expression softening. "You look beautiful..." he says sincerely, then with a playful smirk, adds, "even with your goggles on."

Katie blushes even more, but she can't hide the small smile tugging at her lips.

Watching their interaction, Charlie couldn't help but feel a surge of happiness for his sister. For the first time in a while, he saw a spark in her that had been missing.

The following evening, the warm, inviting glow of the dining room in Jon's mansion creates an atmosphere of comfort and elegance. As Katie and Brock enter, Brandon instantly recognizes him as the man who had pushed Katie's wheelchair to safety. Observing the way Katie introduces Brock, along with the expressions on their faces, Krystal and Brandon feel a profound sense of relief and joy. That same warmth and happiness fills the room when Charlie introduces Amanda to them.

As they step into the dining room, they are surprised to find two unexpected guests: Fraser and Kelsi, seated and engaged in conversation with Jon and Chelsea. The moment Fraser and Kelsi notice them, they rise from their seats.

"Hi, Katie and Charlie. It's great to see you here," Fraser greets warmly, with Kelsi adding, "And these must be your friends?"

After the introductions, Fraser smiles and says, "We've known Jon and Chelsea for nearly ten years. Jon used to run a rehab center that utilized the '*Eyes of an Angel*' program, and we collaborated quite a bit."

Kelsi adds with a warm tone, "The last time we saw Krystal was six years ago. I can hardly believe how much she's grown — she's so stunning now that I didn't recognize her when I saw her at the beach a few days ago."

Fraser smiles humbly. "All under the glory of our Lord," he replies softly. "He's the one who inspires what might seem impossible."

The room grows quiet. The four couples—Krystal and Brandon, Katie and Brock, Chelsea and Jon, Charlie and Amanda—naturally gather closer, drawn into the stillness. There is no performance in Fraser's words, only calm certainty, and it leaves a quiet impression on everyone present.

After a thoughtful pause, Fraser adds gently, "For every event in our lives—if the Lord does not will it to happen, it simply will not happen."

His eyes meet Jon's, then Chelsea's.

They understand immediately. They had walked to the edge of divorce, and it was their daughter's tears that brought them back.

Krystal glances at Brandon, then at Katie. *That was a close one,* she realizes. *If I hadn't been in the hospital, Mom and Dad might never have spoken again.*

Brandon tightens his grip around Krystal's hand, Jon's words from the coffee shop echoing in his mind: *I don't want to see you make the same mistake I did.*

Katie finally speaks, hesitant but sincere.

"Uncle Fraser... when I didn't know what to do, I held the heart pendant you gave me. I wasn't even sure I was making the right choice—but I felt peaceful."

Fraser nods, lifting his cup for a small sip, letting the silence do the work.

Then he chuckles.

"This heart of an angel did absolutely nothing, Katie," he says lightly. "It's just a toy I made for Tiffany's fifth birthday. I thought it was cute, so I made a few extras."

Laughter ripples gently through the room.

But Fraser's expression softens again.

"It wasn't the pendant," he says quietly. "It was the *heart of an angel* in you that made the right decision. The pendant had nothing to do with it."

The words settle over the room—not as a lesson, but as truth.

Katie stares at the pendant in her hand, her cheeks warming with a mix of surprise and humility. The room falls into a reflective silence, Fraser's words lingering in the air. Everyone feels the depth of his wisdom and is inspired by the strength and grace Katie has shown.

Brock feels a quiet calling in Fraser's words. Without hesitation, he frees one hand to wrap around Katie's shoulder. Katie, feeling his warmth, naturally rests her head on his, the gesture speaking volumes without a single word.

He does not fully understand the dynamics of the full story behind everyone. He only knows Katie is tenderly resting her head on his shoulder.

He recalls the bus stop scene, the instant after he ripped her goggles from her face.

And now he understands why that moment unsettled him so deeply.

It wasn't her beauty.

It was the way she chose kindness when she had every reason not to. The way she trusted strength without force. The way she saw him—not as a bully, not as a threat—but as someone capable of choosing better.

Brock exhales slowly.

For the first time, he doesn't feel the need to run ahead of her...or stand in front of her.

Just to walk beside her.

Maybe that's what it means to protect someone.

Not to fight for them. But to become someone worth standing next to.

Seeing the tender moment, Fraser smiles thoughtfully and adds, "When you make the right decision, you are rewarded with something invaluable — something beyond imagination."

His words settle over the room like a blessing, leaving everyone with a sense of peace and gratitude.

Suddenly Amanda, typically as quiet as Charlie, surprises everyone with a playful remark: "Sis Katie, your award was actually waiting for you just a few rooms away that day while you were speaking."

Laughter erupts, filling the room, as Brock and Katie's cheeks flush with joyful embarrassment.

After dinner, they all gather in the living room, chatting comfortably, when Kelsi's phone rings. She excuses herself with a polite smile and steps into the kitchen to take the call.

Meanwhile, Brandon and Brock, both avid martial arts enthusiasts, naturally gravitate toward Charlie.

"Hey Charlie, I saw what you did on the beach. How did you learn to fight like that?" Brandon finally voices the question that's been on his mind for a while.

Charlie shakes his head modestly. "I can't fight, Brandon. It's just defense," he replies, his calm demeanor immediately capturing the attention of both Brandon, Brock, and Krystal too.

"Uncle Jordan said because I rely on my goggles to sense things, I'm not moving as fast as the other guys,"

Charlie admits. He trusts his friends not to exploit his vulnerability. "So he taught me to wait for the right moment — to strike just once, hard enough to disable my opponent." He pauses, a determined glint in his eye. "That's why I've been training for strength."

"You must be working really hard to get to this level," Brock says, nodding with genuine admiration. Then, with a playful grin, he adds, "Though, to be fair, nobody can knock me down with just one move — except you, Charlie."

Charlie's cheeks flush a deep red, and Amanda, noticing his embarrassment, gently loops her arm through his, her smile warm and encouraging.

After a while, Kelsi returns, gives Fraser a knowing wink, and quietly leads Chelsea out of the room.

Jon, unable to hide his curiosity, turns to Fraser. "What's going on? Who called?"

Fraser shrugs casually, a small smile playing on his lips. "No idea," he replies. "But whatever it is, it's good news."

In the bedroom, Kelsi speaks to Chelsea with a mix of excitement and urgency. "Remember my sister Britney? She's now an Ob-Gyn intern at Stanford. She just called."

"Oh, Britney? The prettiest doctor at Stanford?" Chelsea teases, her eyes sparkling with curiosity. "Why's she calling?"

"Remember how you told me about being at high risk for placental abruption with a second pregnancy? I shared that with Brit since she specializes in Ob-Gyn. Turns out, she's been working on a report about this complication with her professors and colleagues."

Kelsi can barely contain her excitement as she continues. "A while back, she told me her team was developing a procedure to lower the risk for mothers. And just now, she called to share an update!"

She pauses to catch her breath, her voice rising with enthusiasm. "She said they've tested the new procedure on three patients so far — and it was successful for all of them! The chances of maternal recovery are now up to 75% !"

Chelsea's face lights up with hope as she quickly leaves the room to bring Jon and Fraser into the bedroom, leaving the younger group to continue their conversations in the living room.

Once Jon enters, Kelsi eagerly recounts her sister's efforts and the breakthrough results.

Jon's expression softens as he turns to embrace Chelsea, his voice low but firm. "But it's still a risk. I can't let you take that chance, Chelsea," he said, though his words carry enough weight for everyone to hear.

Chelsea's voice is gentle yet resolute as she replies, "I'm willing to risk it for you, Jon. I know how much you want to have a child with me. You've told me before that Samantha is willing to be a surrogate, and that's so generous of her. But she's getting married soon. It wouldn't be fair to her or her husband."

Jon falls silent, his eyes searching hers for a moment before both of them look to Fraser and Kelsi.

Fraser steps forward, placing a comforting arm around each of their shoulders. His voice is calm yet unwavering.

"It's not a risk, Jon and Chelsea," he says firmly. "Your love and care for one another, combined with your friend Samantha's selflessness, is proof of something greater. Our Lord listens. Your family has endured so much. Have faith, and He will provide."

They emerge from the bedroom and rejoin the group in the living room.

Krystal immediately notices the smiles on her parents' faces. She doesn't need to ask why — they radiate a quiet joy that tell her something good is about to happen in their family.

As the evening draws to a close and everyone begins preparing to leave, Chelsea suddenly rises from her seat, her eyes sparkling with a gentle idea.

"Before we end this lovely evening," she says warmly, "how about we sing a song together?"

Without hesitation, Kelsi moves to the piano. Her fingers find the keys effortlessly, and the first tender notes of *You Needed Me* fill the room, setting the tone for a perfect ending to the night.

Chelsea begins softly, her voice carrying quiet emotion.
"I sold my soul, you bought it back for me..."

As she sings, her gaze drifts to Jon, her thoughts returning to the many nights she once stood alone on stage.

Jon joins her, smiling at both Chelsea and Krystal as he hums along,
"You put me high, upon a pedestal,
So high that I could almost see eternity..."

Brock tries to keep a low profile, but he can't help himself. Still holding Katie's hand, he joins in quietly,
"And turned my lies back into truth again,
You even called me friend..."

Katie glances at him, unable to resist. Her voice slips in softly, warm and sincere.

178

"Why should I leave, I'd be a fool,
'Cause I've finally found someone who really cares..."

Across the room, Krystal and Brandon exchange a familiar look and sing together, as they always do,
"You gave me strength to stand alone again,
To face the world out on my own again..."

The room fills—not with perfection, but with something far truer: forgiveness, belonging, and choice.

As the final note lingers in the air, Fraser stands silently. His usual composure gives way to a rare moment of vulnerability. Tears glisten in his eyes, though his smile remains steady. He nods gently, his expression speaking louder than words.

It is a night they will all remember—

their hearts connected through music, love, and grace.

~ ~ ~ ~ ~

Epilogue

On the ride home, Charlie and Amanda sit near the front of the bus, talking quietly. Katie is at the back in her wheelchair, Brock beside her, carrying his crutches across his lap.

"Tonight was something," Brock says after a moment. "I could feel the energy, even though I didn't get the whole story."

"I'll explain it to you later," Katie replies, smiling. "But tonight... I'm glad you were there with me."

The bus stops a block from the Santos house.

Brock hesitates, then asks, "Can I see you tomorrow?"

"I'm always at the bus stop in front of Willow Grove at three fifteen," Katie says softly.

The next afternoon, Charlie is in the gym with Amanda, shooting baskets.

Katie waits alone at the bus stop. The regional debate is coming up, and she knows she'll have to face Krystal again. The thought drifts through her mind just as she sees Brock approaching.

This time, he's carrying a backpack stuffed with textbooks—so unlike him that she almost smiles.

"Hi, Brock," she says as he nears. "You look uneasy."

He exhales. "My counselor talked to me today. With my grades, I have to take a high-school exit exam. If I don't pass, I can't graduate."

He looks straight at her. "You know I have to graduate."

"Yes," Katie says, nodding. "You do."

She pauses, then adds, almost without thinking, "If you want, I can tutor you."

The relief on his face is immediate.

For the next couple of months, they meet at Leo's Pizzeria to study together. Neither of their homes feels right, so they choose the place where they first met.

This time, with Brock sitting beside her, no one comes over to interrupt.

Uncle Leo watches them with a knowing smile.

— ✦ —

Six Months Later

The auditorium is already full when Katie reaches the side entrance, the low hum of conversation rolling outward in waves. Caps and gowns fill the aisles like a tide held in place, blue fabric catching the light each time someone shifts in their seat.

She pauses just beyond the curtain, hands resting on the rims of her wheels.

"You ready?" Charlie asks softly.

Katie smiles, just a little. "I think so."

He grins, pride unhidden now, and steps aside as a faculty member approaches, a clipboard tucked against her chest.

"Graduating class," she announces moments later, her voice carrying easily, "please welcome this year's valedictorian—Katie Santos."

Applause rises before the last syllable settles. It isn't explosive. It is steady. The kind that doesn't rush her.

Katie wheels forward.

From the front row, Krystal watches her appear under the lights, posture composed, movement unhurried. Brandon sits beside her, hands folded, eyes fixed on the stage. Brock stands near the aisle, still enough to look rooted. Jon and Chelsea lean together, Chelsea's fingers tightening briefly around Jon's sleeve. A few rows back, Fraser and Kelsi sit shoulder to shoulder, their attention undivided.

Katie reaches the podium and adjusts the microphone once.

"Good morning," she says.

The room grows quiet.

"I was told this speech was supposed to summarize everything we've learned," she begins. "Which felt ambitious—given how often this year reminded me that learning doesn't follow a schedule."

A ripple of gentle laughter moves through the audience.

"This year taught me about preparation," she continues. "About discipline. About standing your ground when you believe in something."

Her eyes lift briefly, finding Krystal's.

"And it taught me about losing."

The word lands softly.

"Some of you know I didn't win my final debate this year," Katie says, calm and unembarrassed. "I wanted to. I was ready. And I lost anyway."

Krystal feels her chest tighten.

"After I lost, I told myself it was about preparation or phrasing. But the truth is simpler."

Katie glances at Brock, who is watching her intently.

"In the middle of my closing, a memory crept in uninvited—of someone who helped me once without knowing my name, without knowing who I was. It had nothing to do with the debate. For a second, I wasn't fully there."

Brock's heart skips a beat.

"I'm sure some of you know that feeling," she adds. "You keep going, you finish what you started—but part of you has already stepped somewhere else."

"I learned something important in that moment," Katie continues. "Not about arguments or judges, but about myself. I learned that disappointment doesn't erase effort. And that not winning doesn't undo who you are."

184

Her gaze lingers on Krystal just long enough to be unmistakable.

Krystal swallows.

Is she saying this for herself...or for me?

The thought unsettles her.

She remembers the weeks after the competition — how she had questioned her own worth beyond trophies and rankings.

Katie never frames the loss as intention. She names it, owns it, and lets it stand. And yet, standing there now, Krystal wonders:

What kind of friendship am I offering, if I'm still measuring it by how it makes me feel?

Katie continues, unaware—or perhaps very aware—of the storm she's stirred.

"For a long time," she says, "I believed that earning respect meant proving myself again and again. That I had to arrive with answers, accomplishments, reasons."

Her hands rest open on the podium.

"What I've learned is that dignity isn't something you earn by outperforming others. It's something you keep by staying honest—about your limits, your hopes, and your losses."

The room listens—not as an audience, but as witnesses.

"We're all leaving here with unfinished things," Katie says. "Dreams that changed shape. Moments that didn't go the way we rehearsed them."

A pause.

"That doesn't mean we failed. It means we're still becoming."

She tilts her head back slightly, then adds, almost as an afterthought:

"And if I've learned anything worth sharing today, it's this—sometimes the bravest thing you can do is let someone else stand tall... and trust that you will, too."

She nods once and wheels back from the microphone.

For a heartbeat, the auditorium is utterly still.

Then the applause rises—surrounding her, lifting—not because she has won everything, but because she has owned all of it.

As she rolls down the ramp, Brock matches her pace without speaking. Charlie laughs through damp eyes, unashamed. Brandon watches her with a new kind of understanding.

Krystal stands quietly.

She claps, too—harder than she meant to—her thoughts tangled and raw.

For the first time, winning doesn't feel like the end of the story.

Backstage is narrower than Katie expects—too many chairs, too many cords taped to the floor. The applause echoes faintly through the walls, softened now into something distant and unreal.

Charlie reaches her first.

"You did it," he says, his voice breaking into a grin. "You actually did it."

Katie laughs. "I talked for six minutes and didn't roll over anyone's foot. I'll take that as a win."

Charlie shakes his head, eyes shining. "I'm proud of you, Sis."

Brandon steps forward, a bouquet of yellow roses in his hands.

"Congratulations, Katie. Valedictorian," he says. "I'm so happy for you."

"Thanks, Brandon." Katie smiles as she holds the bouquet to her chest.

This time the color is right, she thinks. *But is valedictorian the only thing he sees?*

The ache flickers—and is gone.

Krystal hovers a step behind him, uncertain in a way Katie has never seen before.

"That part about losing," Krystal says quietly. "You didn't have to—"

"I wanted to. I know how it sounds," Katie says just as quietly. "But you know my story."

Krystal studies her face—not searching now, just seeing.

"Yeah," she says at last. "I do."

She hesitates, then adds, half-smiling, "On another day, I'm not so sure who would win."

Katie shakes her head lightly. "You would. You were focused and confident. That's what counts."

Krystal swallows, then pulls her into a brief, careful hug.

For a moment, neither of them says anything. Silence speaks more than words ever could.

Fraser approaches with Kelsi, gently breaking the stillness.

"So," he asks, "what comes next for you?"

Katie doesn't answer right away.

She looks at the empty hallway, at the discarded programs on the floor, at the doorway leading back into noise and celebration. Then she looks down at her hands—steady now in a way they hadn't always been.

"I want to be an attorney," she says.

Fraser raises an eyebrow, intrigued but not surprised.

"I want to advocate for justice," Katie continues. "For people who don't get heard. For people who get overlooked because it's easier not to see them."

She meets his gaze fully.

"I don't just want to win arguments," she adds. "I want to change outcomes."

Fraser smiles—not proudly, not sentimentally, but with recognition.

"That," he says, "is who you are."

Katie considers the words, then nods. "It is."

Kelsi squeezes Fraser's hand, eyes warm. "Whatever it is," she says, "you'll be good at it."

Katie smiles, feeling the truth of that settle—not as certainty, but as direction.

As Charlie wheels Katie out toward the courtyard, Brock steps up quickly to catch them.

"Katie, I wasn't there to see you at your debate," he says softly. "I had to prepare for my graduation exam."

He looks at her. "I should be there. But if I flunked that exam, I couldn't graduate."

"You'll pass, Brock," Katie says playfully. "But for me, you can make it up."

"How?" Brock asks.

Charlie, normally quiet, grins. "You can start now by wheeling her."

He passes the wheelchair handles to Brock.

Katie blushes, smiling.

* * * * * * * *

Music Acknowledgment

The following musical works are referenced in *Heart of an Angel* for narrative and emotional context:

You and Me Against the World
Written by Kenny Rogers and Kim Carnes

I Will Always Love You
Written by Dolly Parton

You Needed Me
Written by Randy Goodrum

Author's Afterthoughts

Heart of an Angel was written quietly as the second story of the Angel series. I didn't begin with a message or a lesson in mind. I followed the characters and waited for them to show me who they were, and what they needed to protect. As I wrote, Katie, Charlie, Krystal, and Brandon revealed themselves — along with others who entered the story quietly and stayed.

The heart of an angel is not always easy to see.

Sometimes it appears as courage that stands its ground — choosing kindness over bitterness, dignity over fear. Sometimes it shows itself as generosity that gives without claiming, creating life or hope while asking for nothing in return.

And sometimes, it takes its most difficult form: love that steps aside, choosing absence so that others may live in peace.

They do not ask to be witnessed.

They do not ask to be rewarded.

They do not ask to be remembered.

Writing this story reminded me that not all strength looks like action. Some of it looks like restraint. Some of it looks like patience. And some of it even looks like regret. Yet these choices shape lives all the same.

193

If this story lingered with you — if certain choices felt heavier, quieter, or more costly than others — then you may already know where the heart of an angel was beating.

This book was shaped slowly, and with care. I hope it is read the same way.

— *Francis*